"A month? You're asking me to stay for a whole month?"

"You'd enjoy it."

"I— I—" Nell took a gulp of wine and tried to think straight. "You're not serious, are you?"

"Why not?"

"You can't just drop out of the sky and into my life and say, 'Hey, come live with me'—as if the past twenty years haven't happened."

"I realize that."

"What are you saying, then?"

Jacob's smile did wicked things to Nell's stomach. "I'm saying that we're grandparents of a baby boy who needs us. We're both very keen to be a significant part of his life, and it'll be damned difficult to do that if we're living thousands of kilometers apart. So my invitation makes good sense."

Dear Reader,

I eventually married the lovely man who was my boyfriend when I was nineteen. But most young people of that age move on to form new relationships, and the old boyfriends disappear, never to be heard of or seen again.

In many cases, that's probably a good thing. But I'm sure there are occasional wistful moments when some women wonder, *What if…?*

What if I saw him again after all these years? Would he recognize me? Would he have changed? Would there still be a spark?

What if…? is the question writers ask all the time. It's how we come up with stories. So I guess it's hardly surprising that we love reunions. They're so brimming with tension and questions and romantic potential.

When I first started on this plot possibility, I never dreamed I'd end up writing about Nell and Jacob being brought together by a twist of fate to care for their baby grandson! But the temptation to try something quite different is very alluring, and I was delighted that my editor loved the idea, too.

I hope you enjoy Nell and Jacob's journey to happiness.

Warmest wishes,

Barbara

BARBARA HANNAY

Adopted: Outback Baby

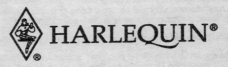

HARLEQUIN®

TORONTO • NEW YORK • LONDON
AMSTERDAM • PARIS • SYDNEY • HAMBURG
STOCKHOLM • ATHENS • TOKYO • MILAN • MADRID
PRAGUE • WARSAW • BUDAPEST • AUCKLAND

ISBN-13: 978-0-373-17526-0
ISBN-10: 0-373-17526-4

ADOPTED: OUTBACK BABY

First North American Publication 2008.

www.eHarlequin.com

Printed in U.S.A.

Barbara Hannay was born in Sydney, educated in Brisbane and has spent most of her adult life living in tropical North Queensland, where she and her husband have raised four children. While she has enjoyed many happy times camping and canoeing in the bush, she also delights in an urban lifestyle—chamber music, contemporary dance, movies and dining out. An English teacher, she has always loved writing, and now, by having her stories published, she is living her most cherished fantasy.

In 2007, Barbara won the Romance Writers of America RITA® Award for Best Traditional Romance, with *Claiming His Family*.

To catch up on all Barbara's latest news, visit www.barbarahannay.com.

From bump to baby and beyond....

Whether she's expecting or they're adopting, a special arrival is on its way!

Follow the tears and triumphs as these couples find their lives blessed with the magic of parenthood....

Don't miss
The Millionaire's Nanny Arrangement
by Linda Goodnight
Coming in October from Harlequin Romance®.

And in December
Pregnant: Father Wanted
by Claire Baxter

PROLOGUE

A SUMMER'S morning at dawn.

Nell and Jacob met at their secret place on the sheltered river bank, the only safe place for the boss's daughter and the hired help.

Arriving by separate tracks, they tethered their horses at opposite ends of the clearing. Nell was nervous and Jacob was on tenterhooks waiting for her news, but he came towards her proudly, striding through the misty morning light with his shoulders back and his head high, as if he owned the earth.

A metre from her, he stopped and she read the silent question in his serious grey eyes.

Too anxious to speak, she simply shook her head, watched the movement in his throat as he swallowed.

'You're pregnant then,' he said quietly.

Nell dropped her gaze to her clasped hands. 'I'm almost certain.' She heard his sharp indrawn breath and whispered, 'I'm sorry.' And she realised for the first time that she was a little afraid of this tall and ruggedly divine young man.

Suddenly, she felt as if she didn't really know him, in spite of the many stolen hours she'd spent with him here during the long, hot weeks of her summer holiday. Pregnancy changed everything, changed something precious and perfect into a shameful mistake. And it forced the two of them to consider a future they weren't prepared for.

More than anything, Nell was scared of what her father would do when he found out. His bad temper was beyond volcanic. He would never forgive her for this and she was certain that he would offer her only one option.

She trembled at the thought, drew a hasty breath for courage. 'My parents will want me to have an abortion.'

Jacob's frown was fierce. 'You don't want that, do you?'

No. She couldn't bear the thought of terminating a baby they had made. She shook her head.

'You mustn't do it then, Nell. Don't even think about it.' He reached for her hands, threaded his strong, work-toughened fingers through hers and she felt the familiar rasp of the callus on his right palm.

Beside them, the river chattered carelessly and the scent of eucalypts and sheoaks hung heavy in the air.

'I'm sorry,' she whispered again.

'Don't be.' Jacob gave her hands a gentle shake. 'Don't apologise.'

Tears stung her eyes. She knew apologies shouldn't be necessary. From the moment she and Jacob had met on that first afternoon, when she'd returned to Half Moon from university, the blame had been equally shared.

She'd seen him tending her father's horses and Cupid had started firing those dangerous little arrows. Their over-the-top attraction had blinded them to anything else, especially to common sense. They hadn't taken precautions that first time.

Now, Jacob gathered Nell in to him and his big hand cradled her head against his shoulder. She adored the smell of him—musky and warm and clean—and something very masculine that she couldn't identify.

He kissed her brow. 'Will you marry me, Nell?'

She gasped, feeling hot and cold with excitement. This was what she'd been longing for, the words from Jacob she'd been silently praying for, secretly clinging to the hope that Jacob would want her and his baby. It was the only way she could possibly face up to her parents.

With trembling fingers, Jacob traced the curve of her cheek. 'I'll look after you, I promise. We'll be all right.'

Oh, yes. They'd be all right. Nell had no doubts. Jacob was an excellent stockman, brilliant on horseback, with a deep love of the land. He would find work anywhere in the Outback. She wouldn't mind too much about giving up her studies and she wouldn't mind about being poor, not if she was with him.

Her parents were the only problem.

They were such painful, *painful* snobs. They'd only sent her to university to snare a rich husband and World War Three would erupt if Nell announced she was marrying their cook's son.

She needed to consider Jacob too, needed to be sure that he was being completely honest. He'd told her about his long-term plans to have his own cattle empire, but that was in the distant future. An early marriage hadn't figured in his scheme.

'Are you sure about this, Jacob?'

With his arms about her waist, he leaned back to look at her and he frowned as if this were a matter of life and death. 'I've never been surer, Nell. I know I don't have much to offer you. You deserve an educated husband, someone rich.'

It was exactly what her parents might say but, coming from him, it sounded wrong. She opened her mouth to protest, but Jacob hurried on.

'I love you, Nell, I swear. And I promise I'll look after you. I'll work hard. I'll get two jobs. I'll make enough money for you and the baby and one of these days we'll have our own place. A big property like Half Moon.'

He was so determined and defiant and Greek god gorgeous he banished her fears as easily as the sun scattered mist.

He said again, 'I love you. You must know that.'

'Yes.' Smiling through happy tears, she wrapped her arms tightly around him. 'And I love you so much it hurts.'

Nell lifted her lips to meet his and they kissed deeply, hungrily. She clung to Jacob, confident that his hard, lean strength would protect her for ever.

'Everything's going to be wonderful,' she said and his face broke into a beautiful grin.

'So you'll marry me?'

'Oh, yes, please. Absolutely.'

'Yes!'

His sudden, joyful whoop startled a flock of finches in a nearby wattle. With another loud shout of triumph, he hoisted Nell high and their laughter mingled with the birds' cries as he spun her around and around in happy circles.

They were going to be married. With their baby, they would be a little family. No one would stop them. All was right with their world.

Jacob slowed before Nell got too dizzy and he let her back to earth, let her body ride slowly...slowly down his muscled length till she reached where he was hard and she almost burst into flames.

Again their mouths met, hungrier than ever. Nell poured her heart and soul into the kiss, wanting him to be certain of how intensely, wildly, completely she loved him.

His hands slipped under her shirt and skimmed lightly over her skin, giving her exquisite shivers.

Abruptly, the stillness of the summer morning was broken by the sound of a cold metallic click.

They froze.

Nell felt Jacob's heart leap against hers as they turned.

Her father stood in the shadows, his face flushed with red fury as he shouldered a shotgun and took aim.

CHAPTER ONE

THE service was over.

Nell knew she must get up and walk outside, but she wasn't sure she could trust her legs to carry her. She had never felt so bereft, didn't know how to cope with the sense of loss.

It was so much worse today than twenty years ago, when they'd taken Tegan away from her. She had been in hospital then, too ill and medicated to fully understand what was happening. This week, a highway smash that rated a thirty-second mention on the six o'clock news had taken her daughter away from her for ever. Today there was nothing to deaden Nell's pain.

Her memories of Tegan were so few. And so cruel. The newborn bundle in her arms, the strong little limbs kicking against the tightly wrapped blanket, just as they had kicked in her womb. The little face and bright, dark eyes. The soft cap of dark hair, the tiny red mouth. The unique, newborn smell of her.

The memories cut into Nell and she wished she could gather her pain around her and disappear completely. It was a blessing, at least, that everyone's sympathy had been showered on Jean and Bill Browne, the couple who had adopted Tegan. Nell knew she must go and speak to them, just as soon as she regained her composure.

'Nell?'

Nell turned stiffly and saw Jean approaching the end of her pew, twisting a damp handkerchief as she peered at her anxiously.

'Jean.' With a hand on the back of the pew for support, Nell struggled to her feet. 'I'm sorry I haven't spoken to you yet.'

The two women—adoptive mother and birth mother— stood, facing each other. Jean Browne looked exhausted, her pale blue eyes rimmed with red, her short grey hair flat and lifeless.

'Please—' The women had met before, on the day after the accident, but now, unable to think clearly, to find the right words, Nell clung to formalities. 'Please accept my condolences.'

Jean's pale eyes swam with tears. 'This is hard for you, too.'

'Yes.' Fighting a dull headache, Nell gathered up her handbag and continued along the pew on unsteady legs. 'I've mentioned this to you before, but I want you to know that I'm very, very grateful to you and Bill. You gave Tegan a wonderfully happy home and—and everything she needed.'

Jean nodded, sent Nell a fleeting, watery smile, then her face crumpled. 'You were such a help the other day. I've been hoping to speak to you. About the baby.'

Nell pressed shaking fingers to her mouth. She'd broken down completely during the eulogy, when the speaker had mentioned Tegan's little son, born just a few short weeks ago.

'I had to leave Sam with a sitter today,' Jean said. 'But I knew that you would like to see him again, especially as Mr Tucker's here as well.'

'Mr Tucker?'

'Tegan's father.'

If Nell hadn't been clutching the back of the pew, she would almost certainly have fallen.

Jacob Tucker was here?

Had he been here throughout the funeral?

An unbearable, thrilling, panicky terror gripped her as Jean flicked a sideways glance back down the aisle. Like the needle of a magnet, Nell whirled around and there was Jacob, standing at the back of the chapel, near the door, tall and stern, with his shoulders back.

His face was partly in shadow but there was no mistaking his chiselled features. All trace of the smooth-skinned boy had vanished, but his strong brows and nose, the handsome cleft in his chin, were still, after twenty years, painfully familiar.

He was wearing a dark suit but, despite the city clothes, the Outback clung to him like a second skin. It was there in the tan on his skin, in the hard-packed leanness of his body, in the creases at his eyes, in the way he stood, poised for action.

And there was a roughness about him now that was unsettling. Devastating.

Nell could still remember with perfect clarity the first time she'd seen him in her father's stables, remembered the shock of attraction that had startled her, enslaved her. She remembered, too, the awful morning on the river bank, the last time she had seen him.

Apart from the occasional photo in cattlemen's magazines—and yes, she'd scanned them regularly, hungry for any news of Jacob Tucker—she knew next to nothing about his life. He'd become a very successful grazier, but there had been no contact between them in twenty years so his private life was a blank.

'I've already spoken to Mr Tucker,' Jean said.

On cue, from the back of the chapel, Jacob offered Nell an unsmiling, almost imperceptible dip of his head.

Her heart pounded. Now she could see the expression in his eyes, the way he looked at her with a mixture of pain and contempt.

She tightened her grip on the back of the pew. With another despairing glance at Jacob, she turned back to Jean. 'I'm sorry. What were you saying?'

'I thought Mr Tucker might like to meet Sam. And I wanted to talk to you both, if possible. I have a problem, you see.'

A stranger, a woman in a green felt hat, bustled into the chapel. 'Oh, there you are, Jean. Sorry, we thought we'd lost you.'

'I won't be long,' Jean told her, then she turned quickly back to Nell. 'I can't talk for very long now. I've got to take Bill home and collect the baby from the sitter. But there's something I need to discuss with you. And Mr Tucker.'

'I—I see.'

Jean blew her nose and darted another glance in Jacob's direction. And now, as if he'd been waiting for some kind of signal, he began to walk towards them.

Nell's breathing faltered. She'd forgotten how big he was, how broad-shouldered and tall, and as his long strides closed the gap between them, she had to look up to see his face. She saw signs of strain in the bleakness of his eyes and in the vertical lines at either side of his grim mouth.

'Hello, Nell.'

'Jacob,' she managed, but her mouth began to tremble.

She was exhausted and dazed and seeing his stern face was almost too much.

He said, 'Mrs Browne has kindly invited me to meet our grandson.'

Our grandson.

Nell wasn't sure which word shocked her more. *Our* suggested that the two of them were still united in some way. *Grandson* hinted at an intimate connection over many, many years, but they were strangers. And not yet forty.

'Maybe this is the wrong time,' Jean said, eyeing them both and sensing their tension. 'I—I have to go. But I couldn't let you both take off without speaking to you.'

'I'm so glad you did,' Nell said, clasping the woman's hand. 'And I'd adore seeing Sam again. That's very kind. We—' She swallowed to ease her choked throat.

'Perhaps you'd rather come separately?' Jean suggested, darting a glance of sharp-eyed curiosity from one to the other.

Nell felt her cheeks grow hot.

'I think we should come together.' Jacob spoke directly to Jean, as if Nell wasn't there. 'You won't want too many interruptions.'

'It would certainly be easier if I could discuss my problem with both of you.'

What was this problem that needed discussing? Nell wished Jean wasn't so evasive, but it certainly wasn't the time to challenge her.

'Would tomorrow morning suit?' Jean asked. 'Will you still be in Melbourne, Mr Tucker?'

'Yes, I'm staying for a few days.'

'At around eleven?'

'Eleven suits me fine.'

'And me,' Nell agreed.

Jean shoved her damp handkerchief into her handbag and snapped it shut as if, somehow, the gesture ended the matter. 'I'll see you then.'

With that she turned and scuttled out of the chapel, clearly relieved to leave Nell and Jacob alone.

Jacob stood at the end of Nell's pew, blocking her exit. She took two steps towards him, as if she expected him to be a gentleman and make way for her, but she was out of luck today. He'd been to hell and back in this chapel, saying farewell to a daughter he had never known, had never held, hadn't so much as touched.

No one here could have guessed or understood how he had loved and missed Tegan, without ever knowing her.

And this woman, whom he'd loved and lost in one short summer, had given their daughter away. So why was she here now, pretending she cared?

'I didn't expect you to be here,' he said between tight lips.

Nell shook her head and she was so close to him, he could smell her perfume, elusive and sweet and unbearably intimate.

'Why wouldn't I come?' Her voice was so choked he could only just catch the words. 'This is our daughter's funeral, Jacob.'

'But you gave Tegan away.'

'No.'

No?

How could she lie? Jacob wanted to confront her, to demand that she retract her lie, but, heaven help him, she looked so vulnerable and tired. Too pale.

Growing paler...

To his dismay, Nell swayed on her feet and sank down

on to the pew, closed her eyes and hunched over, pressing her fingers to her temples. He stared at the top of her golden head and at the play of jewelled lights from a stained glass window throwing red and blue patterns over her.

Her hair was incredibly shiny and so much neater than he remembered. As a girl it had flowed in rumpled waves loose to her shoulders. He reached out a hand, but he didn't touch her. 'Are you OK?'

With her eyes closed, she nodded her head. 'Just tired and sad.'

A moment later, her eyes opened and she turned her head slowly, carefully, almost as if her neck were stiff, and looked up at him. Her blue eyes were lovely—even lovelier than he'd remembered. Looking into them, he felt punch-drunk.

'I really need to go home now,' she said.

Her weakness launched him into gallantry. The questions consuming him would have to wait. 'Of course.'

This time, when he reached down, he touched her sleeve at the elbow. 'Let me drive you.'

Pink stole into her cheeks. 'That's not necessary.'

'Did you bring your car?'

'No,' she admitted reluctantly. 'I came by taxi.'

'Then there's no argument.' His hand closed around her arm and he watched the colour in her cheeks spread. 'Come on.'

To his surprise, she didn't pull away from him, but rose obediently. Everything felt unreal as they walked together out of the chapel into sunshine and fresh air. The mourners had disappeared and the late model Mercedes he'd hired stood alone in the car park.

From a distance of ten paces, Jacob unlocked it. Its lights blinked and Nell gave a little mew of surprise.

'Nice car.'

'It's only hired.' He walked to the passenger's side and opened the door for her, watching every elegant movement as she ducked her head and sat, drawing her slim legs neatly inside. Grimly, he closed her door, walked around the car and got in beside her, wishing he could feel calm.

Keep your mind on the traffic. Forget that it's Nell. And don't think about the past. No sense in dragging her into an argument now.

'Where to?' Jacob asked, forcing cheerfulness into his voice. 'Would you like to go somewhere for coffee?'

Nell shook her head. 'I just need to get home, please.'

'That's in Toorak, right?'

'No.' She quickly donned oversized dark glasses that hid her expressive eyes. 'I don't live there now. I'm in Williamstown.'

Jacob frowned as he started the car and joined the steady stream of traffic. Williamstown was an attractive bayside suburb, but it didn't really make sense that Nell and her barrister husband had moved there. Why would they leave their exclusive address at Toorak, the Melbourne suburb synonymous with opulence and gracious living?

While he was musing over this she asked, 'Where do you live these days?'

'I'm based up in Queensland. Near Roma.'

'That should be good cattle country.'

'Yes, it is.'

'You've done well.'

Unsure if this was a statement or a question, Jacob didn't respond and he drove for some time in uncomfortable silence. Nell sat very straight and still with her hands in her lap, while he kept his gaze strictly ahead.

As they reached the Westgate Bridge arching high over the Yarra River, she asked, 'Did you know about the baby—about Tegan's baby? Before today?'

Jacob turned to her sharply. 'No,' he said. 'I had no idea. Did you?'

She nodded. 'Jean contacted me the day after the accident. She seemed to be struggling with it all and I went over to see if I could help. I saw Sam then. He's very cute.'

'I only found out about Tegan six weeks ago.' It was difficult to keep the bitterness out of his voice.

'So Tegan did write to you?'

'Yes. Quite a long and chatty letter.'

'It must have been a shock.'

He cracked a bitter smile. 'That's something of an understatement. It took me almost a week to recover before I sent my reply.' He paused. 'And then, two days ago, there was another letter from Jean.'

'About Tegan's accident.'

'And details of the funeral arrangements.'

'A much worse shock.'

'Terrible.' After a bit, he said, 'Tegan didn't mention that she was pregnant.'

'But I'm so glad she wrote.'

Jacob frowned. 'You sound as if you were involved somehow.'

Nell dropped her gaze to her handbag—genuine crocodile skin, if he wasn't mistaken. 'Not really.'

'Not really? What does that mean?'

She played with the handle of the handbag, running the tip of her forefinger over the stitching. 'Tegan wrote to me and told me she wanted to make contact with you. I told her what I knew, which wasn't much more than your name and your age. She did the rest. You know how clever young people are on the Internet these days.'

'But she'd already had contact with you?'

'Yes.'

'How? Through an adoption agency?'

'Yes.'

Jacob's hand clenched around the wheel. 'That doesn't make sense. Why couldn't the agency give her my name too?'

When Nell didn't answer, he lost patience. 'Why the hell did *my* daughter have to go to *you* to find out my name?'

'Jacob, be careful!'

A car horn blasted beside them and Jacob realised he'd swerved dangerously close to the next lane. Teeth gritted, he corrected the steering. And then he repeated his question. 'Why did Tegan have to ask you for my name?'

He sent another sharp glance in Nell's direction and, despite the obscuring sunglasses, he saw that her cheeks were flushed, her mouth contorted, embarrassed.

'That's because your name—' The stain in her cheeks deepened. 'Your name wasn't on the records. You—you weren't listed on Tegan's birth certificate.'

'*What?*' The word exploded from him, making Nell flinch.

Too bad, if he'd upset her. She'd upset him. Twenty years of physical exclusion and now the news that there had never been any recognition of his link to Tegan. *Father unknown.* Anger roiled through him, gathering force, an avalanche of emotion.

Beside him, Nell clutched her handbag against her stomach and sat very straight. 'Jacob, we shouldn't discuss this sort of thing while you're driving.'

She was probably right, but his only response was an angry hiss. Jaw clenched, he checked the rear-vision mirror, switched lanes in readiness for the Williamstown exit, and tension, as suffocating as smoke, filled the car's interior.

Five minutes later, Nell directed him into a quiet street a block back from the waterfront.

'My house is the little one over there with the blue door,' she said, pointing.

His anger gave way to bafflement as he pulled up outside a quaint but modest colonial cottage with a front hedge of lavender, a flagstone path and yellow roses over the door. It was the kind of old-fashioned cottage and garden his mother adored, but he'd never dreamed that Nell Ruthven and her husband would live in a place like this.

'Thanks for the lift,' Nell said quietly.

'My pleasure.' Jacob couldn't keep the brittle note out of his voice.

Her fingers sought the door catch.

'Shall I pick you up tomorrow morning to go to the Brownes'?'

After a slight hesitation, she said, 'Thank you. I suppose it makes sense if we travel together.'

'We should talk, Nell.' His mind was still seething with angry questions.

Her eyes met his and he saw a heart-wrenching mixture of sorrow and bewilderment and something deeper he couldn't quite pinpoint.

'After all this time, we have things to say to each other,' he said.

'I can't talk now, Jacob. There's no point in even trying to talk today. We're both too upset and tense.'

Although he was desperate to get everything out in the

open, he had to admit that he felt wrung out. And Nell looked far worse.

She pulled the catch, the door clicked open and the scent of lavender drifted in to him on a light sea breeze. In the distance he could hear a seagull's cry.

'It must be very pleasant living here,' he said in a more conciliatory tone.

'Yes, I love it.' She turned to speak over her shoulder, without quite looking at him. 'Why don't you come early tomorrow? We can talk before we go to the Brownes'?'

'Great idea. We can go for coffee somewhere in the city.'

'We can talk here if you like.'

Jacob frowned. 'Are you sure your husband won't mind?'

He was watching her profile carefully, saw her mouth curl into a complicated, off-kilter smile. 'That won't be a problem. There will only be the two of us. What time would you like to come?'

'Nine? Half past?'

'Make it half past. I'll see you then.'

Nell got out and closed the door behind her and Jacob watched her through the passenger window as she crossed the footpath and opened the front gate. A sudden breeze gusted up the street, shaking the heads of the lavender and, as she walked up the path, the wind teased a bright strand of her hair from its braid and lifted the collar of her jacket against her neck. Her high heels made a tapping sound on the paving stones.

Framed by cream and yellow roses, she stood on her front porch in her neat, dark suit and fished in her handbag for her door key, and she looked beautiful and citified and completely removed from the horse-riding country girl he'd known for two months of one summer twenty years ago.

Tomorrow.

Tomorrow he would be entering that house, talking to Nell at last, discovering the truth he both longed for and feared.

He flipped the key in the Mercedes's ignition so hard he almost snapped it in two.

CHAPTER TWO

Two o'clock in the morning found Jacob awake in his unfamiliar hotel bed.

A picture of Tegan had been displayed at the funeral—his first, his only sight of his daughter—and it haunted him.

She'd been dancing on a sunlit beach and wearing a blue cotton dress that was a perfect match for the bright summer sky. Her feet had been bare and sandy, her tanned arms uplifted, her skirt billowing behind her in the wind. She'd been laughing and her long brown hair had streamed like a dark ribbon. Her eyes had sparkled with the sheer joy of being alive.

Jacob had been startled by how intensely and immediately he'd felt connected to her. The bond had gone beyond the uncanny likeness to his family in the darkness of her hair, the strong lines of her cheekbones, her straight, dark eyebrows. He'd felt it deep in his bones, in his blood, in his breath.

He had, of course, seen Nell in Tegan, too. She'd been there in the tilt of the girl's head, in the slender shapeliness of her long legs. And that led him to thinking about Nell Ruthven née Harrington, about their meeting today. After so long.

He'd been way too tense. Everything about it had been wrong.

So many times during the past twenty years, he'd imagined a parallel universe in which he'd met Nell again. He had never deliberately sought her out, not once he'd learned she was married, but he'd imagined a scenario where they would bump into each other quite by chance. They would drop whatever they had planned for that day and go somewhere just to talk.

They'd smile a lot and chat for ages, catching up. Their reunion would be so poignant that time and Nell's marriage to another man would become meaningless.

'I want to go on seeing you,' he'd say.

She'd smile. 'I'd love that.'

Problem was, this fantasy was based on the twenty-year-old assumption that Nell had been wrong about her pregnancy, that it had simply been a case of a late period. Jacob knew through gossip his mother had passed on that Nell's adult life had never included a child and he'd never dreamed their baby had been given away for adoption.

Tomorrow was going to be difficult. He had questions that demanded answers, but it would also be his one chance to enter that parallel universe, to reconnect with Nell's world. And, even if it was only for a day, he didn't want to get it wrong.

It would be easier to stay calm if he wasn't plagued by bitter-sweet memories of their amazing, devastating summer at Half Moon, if he couldn't still remember painful details of those two short months with Nell, right back to his first sight of her.

Home from university, she had been riding Mistral, a grey mare, and she'd come into the stables where he'd been working. Her cheeks had been flushed from the wind, her eyes bright and she'd been dressed like a glamorous, high-society equestrian in a mustard velvet jacket, pale cream jodhpurs and knee high, brown leather boots.

The fancy clothes had fitted her snugly, hugging the roundness of her breasts, cinching her waist and accentuating the length of her legs. Her pale hair had rippled like water about her shoulders and her eyes had been as blue and clear as icy stars. She had been beautiful. So incredibly beautiful…

But what had happened next was one of those unbelievably zany moments that should only have happened in B grade movies. Nell was leading her horse when she saw him and stopped. And instead of exchanging polite hellos, they'd stood there, open-mouthed, staring at each other, while Jacob's blood had rushed and roared and his heart had become a sledgehammer.

Looking back, he guessed they must have spoken, but the rest of that afternoon was a blur to him now. Much clearer was their meeting the next morning.

He'd gone to the stables just after dawn and noticed immediately that Mistral was missing. He'd guessed that Nell had taken her for an early morning ride and within a dozen heartbeats he'd mounted another horse and taken off.

Half Moon was a huge property and he had no idea where Nell was, but he'd been quite sure at the outset that he would find her, that she'd wanted him to find her. Perhaps the mysterious sixth sense that the gods bestowed on destined lovers had whispered that she would be waiting for him.

It wasn't long before he'd found her horse tied to a tree beside the river where white mist lifted in curling, wispy trails from the smooth, glassy surface of the water.

'Hey there, Jacob.'

Nell's voice seemed to come from a paperbark tree and when he peered through the weeping canopy he saw her sitting on a branch overhanging the water. She was wearing a blue checked shirt and ordinary blue jeans this morning, and dusty, elastic-sided boots. Apart from the golden gleam of her hair, she looked more like the everyday Outback girls Jacob was used to.

'G'day,' he called up to her as he tied his horse's reins to a sapling. 'Looks like you've found a good perch.'

'It's gorgeous out here. Come and see for yourself.'

He laughed and shook his head. 'I don't think that branch would hold the two of us.'

She bounced lightly. 'Oh, it's strong enough. Come on, the river looks so pretty at this time of the morning and I can see right around the bend from here.'

Talk about spellbound. There was no way he could have resisted Nell's invitation.

Knot-holes in the tree's trunk made it easy for Jacob to climb to her branch. He stepped on to it gingerly, pausing to test that it could take his weight. So far, so good, but the branch narrowed quickly.

Nell smiled, her blue eyes dancing with merriment, her white teeth flashing. 'Dare you to come right out.'

She was flirting with him.

And he loved it.

Arms extended for balance, he made his way along the branch. His extra weight sent the leaves at Nell's end dipping into the tea-coloured water, but she only laughed.

'No fancy jodhpurs this morning?' he asked as he got closer.

She screwed up her nose. 'They were a birthday present

from my parents. I only wore them yesterday to please them, but they made me feel such a poser.'

'You looked terrific,' he insisted, taking another step closer. 'You'll wear them to the picnic races, won't—'

A loud crack sounded and the branch exploded beneath them, sent them plummeting into the river.

It was summer so the water wasn't very cold. Jacob fought his way to the surface, looked about for Nell and panicked when he couldn't see her. Heart thrashing, he dived again into the murky green depths. Where was she? He prayed that she hadn't been hit by the falling tree branch.

Lungs bursting, he broke the surface again. Still no sign of Nell. Was she pinned to the river bed?

Once more Jacob dived, groped in the grass and the submerged branches at the bottom, desperate to find her, but again he was forced back to the surface, empty-handed.

'Jacob!'

Thank goodness. He turned to see her breast-stroking towards him.

'I've been looking for you,' she said. 'I was worried that you'd drowned.'

'I thought *you'd* drowned. I was looking for you.'

They swam to the bank. Jacob reached it first and, because it was steep and bare, he offered his hand to help her out. She accepted gratefully and they began to climb.

The bank quickly turned slippery beneath their wet boots and they had quite a scramble. As they neared the top, Jacob grabbed at a sapling for an anchor and pulled Nell towards him.

She came faster than he expected, bumped into him, in fact, and suddenly they were clinging together, her soft curves pressing in to him through their wet clothes. Her clear eyes and parted lips were mere inches from his and, despite the wet hair plastered to her skull, she was beautiful. Breathtakingly so.

She smiled. 'Now this is a new way of breaking the ice. My college social club would be impressed.'

He wasn't sure what she was talking about, but he understood very well the invitation in her eyes. And so he kissed her.

It wasn't a long kiss and it shouldn't have been a sexy kiss. Their lips were cold from the river and Jacob was clinging to the sapling's trunk with one hand while he held Nell to prevent her from falling.

But it was a kiss Jacob would never, to the end of his days, forget. From the moment their lips met, he adored the feel and the taste of Nell, loved her response—so feminine, so...*right*.

Too soon their wonderfully intimate hello was over and he boosted Nell up over the rim of the bank and came after her, tumbling on to the grass.

He might have kissed her again, but they were apart now and he lost his nerve, remembered that she was the boss's daughter and he was the cook's son.

Instead, they lay in the grass at the top of the bank and let the morning sun stream over them, and Jacob contented himself with admiring her breasts, gorgeously outlined by her wet shirt.

'So tell me about your college social club,' he said.

'Oh, they're always coming up with new ways to get everyone to mix.' Nell sat up and lifted her wet hair from the back of her neck. 'They've run a series of cocktail parties where girls and guys can meet, but we're only allowed eight minutes or so to chat with each person and to tell them about ourselves—just enough time to figure out whether people click.'

'Sounds…racy.'

Nell grinned coyly, leant sideways and squeezed water from her hair into the grass. 'Not really. It's only chatting, after all.'

Considering that he'd just kissed her, he supposed she had a point.

'So when you were at one of these parties,' he said, 'you would have said something like—I'm Nell Harrington, I'm nineteen and I'm studying Arts. I like horse riding, apple crumble with cream and sitting in trees.'

Her blue eyes widened. 'How did you know about the apple crumble?'

'My mum was asked to make it especially for your homecoming.'

'Oh, yes, of course. I like Maggie. My mother says she's the best cook we've ever had.'

'I'm not surprised.'

Suddenly the stupidity of this meeting hit Jacob like a smart bomb. What in blue blazes was he doing here chatting with Nell Harrington? Her father would have him neutered if he ever found out.

He jumped to his feet, grabbed his horse's reins. 'I have to get to work.' With luck, the sun and a fast ride would dry his clothes and no one would be any the wiser.

Nell smiled up at him, all sweetness and dimples. 'Do you think we should try for another date?'

That moment had been his chance. He should have told her, No, not on your Nelly, and changed the course of their history, saved decades of heartache. Should have got the hell out of there.

Now, twenty years later, Jacob winced as he remembered how crazily spellbound he'd been.

'I'll see what I can manage,' he'd said.

Nell studied her reflection in the bathroom mirror. Jacob would be here in five minutes and she looked a fright. The ordeal of yesterday followed by a sleepless night had left her pale and haggard, as dreary and limp as wet seaweed.

Dabbing concealer into the shadows under her eyes, she told herself that it didn't matter what she looked like. Jacob's regard for her had disappeared long ago, well before the turn of the twenty-first century.

Despite his controlled good manners yesterday, he'd made it painfully clear that he blamed her, probably despised her. She'd seen it in his eyes, had heard it in his voice and when he'd accused her of giving Tegan away, she'd been too stunned and numb to defend herself. Now he believed he had the high moral ground. For that reason alone she needed to gain some self control. And she needed to look OK.

Taking more than usual care, she lengthened her lashes with mascara, applied blusher to bring colour into her cheeks and selected her favourite lipstick. She ran her fingers lightly through her freshly washed hair, letting it fall loosely to her shoulders, took a step back from the mirror and drew a deep breath.

Her make-up and hair were OK and her floral top and blue skirt were cheery and feminine.

'You'll do,' she told her reflection. She actually looked close to normal now.

If only she *felt* composed. She was no more prepared to 'chat' with Jacob today than she had been yesterday after the funeral. She hadn't been able to stop thinking about him. About Tegan. About Tegan's baby, Sam.

Her mind buzzed like a bee in summer, darting frantically with no clear course. One minute she was drowning beneath the loss of her daughter, the next she was wildly, guiltily excited about the reappearance of Jacob after twenty years, and then she was sobered by the thought of her baby grandson and Jean Browne's mysterious need to discuss *something*.

Nell had telephoned the Brownes the day after Tegan's death. Desperately distressed, she'd needed to talk to them and she'd found comfort from being able to offer help. Bill Browne had suffered a stroke a few months earlier and poor Jean was carrying a huge burden, dealing with her grief while caring for him and the tiny baby, Sam.

Nell had done the little she could—a chicken casserole, help with finding a solicitor. She'd even minded Sam while Jean had dealt with the funeral directors. In a bonding moment over a cup of tea in the Brownes' kitchen, she'd told Jean the circumstances of Tegan's birth.

They'd cried together.

If Jean needed more help now, Nell knew she would be happy to lend a hand. She was less certain about Jacob.

Overnight, every forbidden memory of her youthful lover had shot to the surface—memories of the river, of the endless conversations she and Jacob had shared, of that first morning, sitting on the tree branch, falling into the water.

She and Jacob had even read poetry together. Fresh from her first year at university, she'd been mad about Yeats. She hadn't expected a rugged cowboy to be interested in poetry, had been gobsmacked when Jacob had brought a copy of Yeats that had belonged to his father.

They'd read selections to each other and she'd loved listening to Jacob's deep voice rumbling sexily against a backdrop of chuckling water and softly piping finches.

Good grief. She shouldn't be remembering such things after all this time. But every memory of Jacob Tucker was alive and vivid in her head—his shy, serious smile, the sexy power of his body, his gentle hands.

When she closed her eyes she could still see him lying in the shaded grass, one arm curved above his head, throwing a shadow over his beautiful face. She could see him looking at her from beneath heavy lids. Could see the thrilling intensity of his grey eyes, feel the warmth of his lips on hers.

Nell forced her eyes open again, blinked hard, shook her head. It was both fruitless and painful to revisit the past.

She and Jacob had each gone down separate paths. She'd married Robert Ruthven and Jacob had acquired a cattle kingdom. They'd grown older, richer, wiser and had become very different adults.

Yet here they were, brought back together by the very thing that had separated them in the first place.

Their daughter.

The front doorbell rang and she jumped. *That will be Jacob.*

She wondered what they were going to talk about till it was time to go to the Brownes', and cast another frantic glance at the mirror.

Come on, Nell, you have to try harder than that. Chin up, back straight. Smile.

The smile was problematic, but at least her reflection looked a tad more determined as she hurried to open the door.

Jacob stood on her front doorstep. 'Good morning,' he said, smiling.

Nell's insides tumbled helplessly. 'Morning.'

Silly of her, but she'd been expecting him to look the way he had yesterday, all formal and serious and nudging forty. Today he was wearing faded jeans that clung low on his narrow hips and a navy-blue T-shirt that hugged his whipcord muscles. Apart from the fine lines at the corners of his eyes and the tiniest smattering of grey at his temples, he looked dangerously—way too dangerously—like the nineteen-year-old she'd fallen in love with.

'How are you feeling today?' he asked.

'Much better, thanks.' She almost confessed to not sleeping too well, but decided against giving too much away.

With an offhand smile, he held out a brown paper bag. 'Some comfort food from the bakery.'

'Oh, thank you.' As she took the bag his fingers brushed hers and the brief contact sent a strange current shooting up her arm. *Get a grip, Nell.* Now wasn't the time to become girlish and coy.

'Take a seat in here,' she said, indicating the cosy living room that opened off her front hallway. 'I'll make some tea. Or would you prefer coffee?'

'Tea's fine.' Jacob ignored her instruction and followed her down the hall and into the kitchen.

Flustered, Nell rushed to fill the kettle. It felt so strange to have Jacob Tucker in here, leaning casually against her butter-yellow cupboard with his long denim legs crossed at the ankles, arms folded over his strapping chest.

He looked about him with absorbed interest. Or was that *amused* interest? Was that a smirk she detected? What was so funny? Why couldn't he have waited in the living room, as she'd asked?

Lips compressed, Nell grabbed scarlet and yellow

floral mugs from an overhead cupboard and set them on a wicker tray. She shot him a curious glance. 'Is something amusing you?'

'I was just revising my impressions of you. You haven't changed as much as I thought you had. Yesterday you looked so different in that efficient suit and with your hair all pinned up, but today you're more like the girl I used to know.'

His thoughts were so close to her own that she almost blushed. Her hand trembled as she reached for the teapot. *Don't be fooled. Remember, this isn't a proper reunion. Jacob's filling in time till we see Sam. Nothing more.*

She turned and fetched milk from the fridge, filled a small blue jug. 'I don't think the girl you remember exists any more,' she said quietly.

'I guess looks can be deceiving.'

I should remember that, too.

Nell selected a pretty plate and arranged the biscotti he'd bought at the bakery, set it with the other things on the tray. Turning to him, she said, 'Can you take this tray through to the living room? I'll bring the teapot in a minute.'

'Sure.'

As he left the kitchen, she drew a deep breath and let it out slowly. Behind her the kettle came to the boil.

One look at Nell's living room and Jacob knew that something very important was missing from Koomalong, his Outback homestead. He'd paid a great deal of money for a top Brisbane decorator to furnish his home and she'd gone to enormous trouble to give it a 'masculine edge'.

'A man like you needs an environment that screams alpha male,' the decorator had insisted.

He'd always lived alone, changing women as often as

the seasons, so a 'masculine edge' had made sense. But, despite the expense and the Brisbane decorator's expertise, the so-called alpha male decor hadn't really worked for him. His place didn't feel like a home; it seemed to belong in a glossy city magazine.

The Ruthvens' cottage, on the other hand, felt very homelike indeed. There was something about Nell's living room, about the lounge furniture upholstered in muted creams and dusty reds, that invited him in. The slightly cluttered casualness, the deceptively careless mix of colours and florals and stripes enticed him to relax, to feel welcome.

No doubt the cosy effect was completed by the marmalade cat curled in a sunny spot among fat cushions on the cane sofa beneath the window.

Jacob set the tray down beside a vase of red and cream flowers on an old timber chest that apparently served as a coffee table. A thick paperback novel had been left there and, beside it, elegant blue-framed reading glasses.

Nell wears reading glasses now.

He knew that shouldn't bother him, but somehow he couldn't help being saddened by such a clear marker of the passage of time.

The cat opened its pale yellow eyes and stared at him as he selected one of the deep and friendly armchairs and sat. Almost immediately, the cat rose, stretched its striped orange back, then leapt daintily off the sofa and crossed the floor to jump into Jacob's lap.

As a general rule, he preferred dogs to cats and he eyed the animal dubiously as it balanced on his thighs, a small claw penetrating his denim jeans.

'Don't expect me to let you have this milk, mate.'

In response, the cat dropped softly into his lap, curled

contentedly and began to purr, adding the final brush-stroke to Jacob's impression of Nell's cottage as cosiness incorporated.

Unfortunately, he was particularly susceptible to cosiness. His childhood had been lonely. He and his mother had lived in a series of workers' cottages on Outback properties and he'd longed for the permanence of a cosy family home. There had been several times during the past twenty years when he'd been on the brink of getting married simply so he could enjoy the pleasures of a comfy home and family life.

But whenever he'd come to the point of proposing marriage, something had always held him back—a vital, missing *something*.

'Oh, heavens, Ambrose, what do you think you're doing?' Nell came into the room carrying a blue china teapot. 'I'm sorry about the cat,' she said. 'Shoo, Ambrose. You should have sent him away, Jacob.'

'I would have if he'd bothered me.' Jacob watched the cat return to the sofa, tail waving sulkily. 'Perhaps he's mistaken me for your husband.'

A strange little laugh broke from Nell as she set the teapot down beside the tray. 'No, I'm sure he hasn't. Robert and Ambrose never got on.' She looked flushed and avoided meeting his gaze, rubbed her palms down the sides of her skirt as if they were damp. 'How—how do you take your tea?'

'Black, no sugar.'

'Oh, of course, I remember now.'

As she said this, she looked dismayed and he was dismayed too, suddenly remembering the camp fires down by the river when they'd made billy tea, hastily putting the fire out as soon as the water boiled so that the smoke wouldn't give away their hiding place.

There was a tremor in her hands as she poured his tea and set the mug in front of him. She was nervous and he wanted to put her at ease.

'This is a lovely home,' he said. 'Did you decorate it?'

Nell nodded and concentrated on pouring her own tea, adding milk and a half teaspoon of sugar.

'You must have an artistic eye.'

'Actually, I do seem to have a way with fabric.' She smiled as she settled into the other armchair. 'I make quilts and I sell them.'

'You sell them?'

'Yes. There's quite a demand for my work, actually. It keeps me rather busy.'

Jacob swallowed his shock. But perhaps he shouldn't be so surprised. After all, apart from the gossip his mother gleaned from the social pages, he knew next to nothing about Nell Ruthven. He'd always supposed she was a carefree and idle society wife. One of those ladies who lunched.

But Nell Harrington, the girl he'd loved, had been crazy about poetry, an artistic soul.

'Your husband must be very proud of you,' he said cautiously.

Looking more nervous than ever, Nell picked up her mug of tea, then seemed to change her mind and set it down again.

'How Robert feels about my quilting is irrelevant,' she said quietly. 'He's not my husband any more.'

CHAPTER THREE

'WE'RE divorced,' Nell told Jacob in her quietest, most matter-of-fact voice. Even so, she could see his shock.

'Why—' He lifted a hand to his neck as if he wanted to loosen his collar, but he wasn't wearing one. 'Why didn't you tell me that yesterday? I asked about your husband.'

With a heavy sigh, she said flatly, 'You would have wanted to ask more questions. I couldn't have coped just then.' Embarrassed now, and tenser than ever, she chewed at her lip.

'What about now?' Jacob demanded. 'Could you cope with questions now?'

Keeping her gaze fixed on the tea tray, she shook her head. 'Don't bother with the questions. I'll tell you. Our marriage didn't work. It was as simple as that. There was nothing nasty. Robert worked too hard and drank too much, but he never hurt me. We just drifted apart and I've been divorced for nearly a year.'

She tried to make light of it, but it wasn't easy to shrug off. She could hardly admit that after losing Jacob she'd married the wrong man, that too late she'd realised that Robert had simply wanted her as a trophy wife. He'd been happy to be seen with her at all the important functions around Melbourne but, in the privacy of their bedroom, their relationship had never really clicked.

'Robert had so many legal colleagues, we were able to settle things quite easily,' she said. 'It was all very straight-forward and extremely civilised. The marriage might not have been a success, but the divorce was a triumph.'

'What do you mean?'

Lifting her chin, she tried to smile. 'I mean I'm now in charge of my life. For the first time ever, I'm independent and in control.'

Jacob nodded, but his eyes remained cold.

Embarrassed, she reached for her mug and took a long drink of tea. Her heart thumped and she held the mug with two hands so the tea didn't spill. Perhaps it was too much to expect Jacob to understand why she'd stayed too long in an empty marriage, that after losing her daughter she'd desperately hoped to avoid another failure.

'What about you?' She forced the question. 'Are you married?'

He shook his head. 'Never tempted.'

There was a glint in his eyes which she quickly avoided.

'I'm a well-seasoned bachelor,' he said.

Was he telling her that he was available? A wave of heat rolled over her. For heaven's sake. What on earth was the matter with her? Bending forward, she picked up the plate and offered it to him. 'Biscotti?'

'Not now, thank you.' Jacob's fingers drummed on the upholstered arm of the chair. 'So you've already seen Tegan's baby?'

'Yes, he's a lovely little fellow. He must be about seven weeks by now.'

'Seven weeks? They're still pretty small at that age, aren't they?'

She couldn't help smiling. 'Yes, quite small. Why?'

'Oh, I can't help being curious about what Jean wants to discuss. It's obviously something to do with Sam.'

Nell nodded. 'He must be a handful for Jean, especially when her husband's so incapacitated.'

'What's the matter with her husband?'

'He had a stroke last April.'

'Poor man. They are certainly going through a terrible time.' Jacob's eyes narrowed as he watched her. 'So will you be taking any interest in Sam?'

'What makes you ask that? Of course I'm interested in him. He's my grandson.'

His eyes were cold. 'You weren't interested in his mother.'

He couldn't have hurt her more if he'd tripped her, sending her flat on her face. 'How dare you?'

'It's the truth, Nell. You gave Tegan up for adoption.'

'Not me—'

Jacob steamrolled over her protest. 'And for nineteen years that poor girl was led to believe that I couldn't give a damn about her.'

To Nell's dismay, Jacob leapt to his feet and towered over her.

'You've deprived me of my daughter. Why on earth did you do that, Nell?'

'You know that's not fair.' Her hands fisted so tightly her nails dug into her palms. She wanted to leap to her feet too, but how ridiculous that would be. A sparring match. 'Have some pity,' she cried, looking up at him. 'You don't know what happened. You don't know what I've been through.'

He stood with his hands clenched at his sides, his jaw jutting at a stubborn angle.

With calm emphasis on each word, Nell said again, 'You don't know what happened.'

Jacob's mouth opened as if he was about to burst out with another angry accusation, but as he stood there, staring at her, she could see that her words were taking hold. The anger in his eyes lessened, confusion returned.

Sinking his hands into the pockets of his jeans, he looked chastened. 'I'm sorry. I was just letting off steam.' He returned to the armchair, lifted the mug of tea and stared at it. 'Can you tell me exactly what happened?'

Nell couldn't hold back a despairing sigh. 'I can't believe you think I could willingly give my daughter away.'

'Our daughter.'

'Yes, Jacob. Our daughter.'

He set the mug down. 'Until Tegan wrote to me, I didn't even know you'd given birth. Later, when I'd heard you and your husband referred to as childless, I assumed you'd had a miscarriage. Or an abortion. I thought there was even a chance that you'd never been pregnant at all, that you'd been mistaken.'

Nell swallowed. 'I'm so sorry you never knew.'

'Believe me, so am I.' He shifted forward in his chair, eyed her levelly. The muscles in his throat worked. 'I can't help feeling cheated.'

'I know,' Nell said softly. She'd felt cheated too—cheated out of motherhood. But at least she'd known where Tegan was, that she was safe and happy. '*I* didn't give Tegan away, Jacob. You must remember what my parents were like.'

He watched her with calculated wariness. 'I know your

father held a gun to my head. I know he forced my mother and me to leave Half Moon without collecting our wages.'

'And he sent me down here to Melbourne to a private Home for unmarried mothers.'

The hardness fell from Jacob's face. 'All the way down here?'

'Yes.'

'No wonder I couldn't find you.'

'Did you try to find me?'

'Of course I tried. I was desperate to find you. We'd planned to be married, remember?'

His eyes shimmered and Nell's heart stumbled.

'I couldn't find you either,' she admitted. 'I tried, but I wasn't allowed many phone calls from the Home. I tried again after Tegan was born. I rang everyone I could think of. Someone mentioned that you'd gone interstate, but no one knew where. You and your mother just disappeared into the Outback.'

When he made no comment, she felt compelled to ask, 'Do you believe me, Jacob?'

He nodded grimly. 'My story's much the same. I went to your university. I found people who knew you, but they couldn't tell me where you were.'

'I never went back to university.'

A shuddering sigh escaped him. He cleared his throat. 'So was Tegan born here, in Melbourne?'

'Yes. I won't burden you with details, but it was a difficult birth and I was in a bad way afterwards. They kept me heavily sedated.'

Jacob swore softly.

'When my parents gave me papers to sign, I didn't understand that I was giving the baby up for adoption.'

'But that's criminal.'

Choked by memories, Nell nodded again. She'd relived that day countless times. 'I thought I was just signing papers for the baby's birth certificate.'

It hurt to talk about this. A sob burned her throat but she stumbled on, needing to tell him everything. But, more than anything now, she wanted to share with him her precious memories of their daughter.

'Tegan was gorgeous, Jacob. When she was born, she was so tiny and perfect and cute. She had such a sweet face. Gorgeous dark eyes—a bit unfocused, of course. And her little pink fingers were curling over the edge of her blanket and she had the most perfect miniature fingernails.'

Avoiding the pain in his face, she closed her eyes. *Don't cry. It won't help anyone if you cry.* She drew a deep breath. 'I didn't know that was the last time I would see her.' She drew another breath for courage. 'They told me they were putting her in some kind of foster care until I was fully recovered.'

'Nell.'

'I broke down completely when I realised what I'd signed, but the nurse in charge just whacked me with more sedatives.'

'How could she?'

'It was twenty years ago. Anything could happen if someone paid enough money.'

A growl of rage broke from him.

'Afterwards, Mum and Dad whisked me back to Queensland and no one ever told me that I had thirty days to change my mind about the adoption. As soon as I was strong enough, I left Half Moon, but by the time I got back down here it was too late to reclaim Tegan.'

Hands fisted, Jacob sat very still, staring at her, his eyes dark with raw pain, his throat working overtime.

'As far as I'm concerned, my daughter was stolen from me,' Nell said finally. 'And there hasn't been a day—not a day—in the past twenty years when I haven't thought about her, when I haven't missed her.'

He nodded bleakly and Nell sensed that it was beyond him to speak at that moment. For quite some time he sat very still, his elbows propped on the arms of the chair, his profile showing no expression, his eyes downcast. The room seemed to hum with a thousand unspoken thoughts.

Finally, he asked, 'Is there any particular reason why you and Robert didn't have any children?'

His question was so unexpected that Nell blurted out the truth. 'Robert wasn't very interested in having a family. And I was happy enough to go along with that. Another pregnancy would have made me relive everything I went through with Tegan. I was trying to forget.'

'Forget?'

'Not Tegan. I certainly didn't want to forget her. But I had to find a way to move on.' When he didn't reply, she added, softly, 'I've wondered if you were trying to forget too, if that's why you've worked so hard for all these years.'

His eyes flashed with sudden surprise. 'How do you know I've worked hard?'

She laughed guiltily. 'I've read the occasional article in cattlemen's magazines.'

'You know they always exaggerate.' Jacob looked uncomfortable, glanced at his wristwatch. 'Hmm…how far is it to the Brownes' place?'

'Oh, it will probably take us about twenty minutes.'

'I suppose we'd better get going, then.'

'Yes.' As Nell gathered their tea things and stacked them on the tray, she felt unsettled. They'd spent the whole time talking about her and she hadn't learned anything about Jacob.

He said, 'We may as well take my car.'

'That suits me, thanks. I'll just pop these things back in the kitchen and get my bag.'

She was rather stunned to discover a huge bouquet of beautiful stargazer lilies on the back seat of Jacob's car and a brightly coloured, stuffed Humpty Dumpty.

'No prize for guessing which is for Jean and which is for Sam,' Jacob said with a sudden grin.

'That's very thoughtful, Jacob. I'm afraid I didn't think to get anything today.'

'These can be from both of us then.'

It was silly to feel so pleased, but she couldn't help it when Jacob smiled. 'The flowers must be from you,' she said. 'It will make Jean's day if she receives a bouquet from a handsome younger man.'

'Younger?' Jacob's eyes gleamed as he shook his head at her. 'I'm a granddad, you know.'

'Oh, yes.' Good heavens, they weren't flirting, were they? 'How could I forget?'

He opened the door for her but, before she could get in, his hand curved around the back of her neck and he turned her face towards him and kissed her, very lightly, on the mouth.

'Just curious to know what it's like to kiss a granny,' he murmured.

He rounded the car and slipped into the driver's seat as if nothing out of the ordinary had happened, but as they drove to the Brownes' Nell felt light-headed, almost dizzy.

* * *

Jean Browne must have been waiting for them because the door opened before they could knock. She looked terribly tired. Her grey hair hung limply and her dress was crumpled and there was a damp patch on her shoulder. Nell wondered if the baby had caused it.

When Jacob offered Jean the bouquet, her pale eyes welled with instant tears. 'Oh, how lovely.'

'I didn't want to come empty-handed,' he said. 'You've done so much for our daughter.'

Nell knew her heart wasn't supposed to flip at the way Jacob said 'our', as if they were still—had always been—a couple.

'Thank you so much. They're beautiful.' Jean buried her nose in the flowers and for a moment she looked quite girlish. 'Don't they smell wonderful? And how clever of you to guess that lilies are my favourite. Bill always buys them on my birthday.'

Her cheeks turned as pink as the lilies as she sent a fond glance back over her shoulder to her husband, who was sitting quietly in an armchair in the far corner. He was older than Jean, thin and balding with a fringe of white hair. His eyes were closed and he seemed to be asleep.

Lowering her voice, she said to Jacob, 'I didn't like to mention it yesterday, but Bill had a stroke five months ago. He's lost the use of his right arm and he still can't talk very well. He's a bit wobbly on his pins too, poor love.'

'That's very bad luck.'

'It's very frustrating for him,' Jean told them. 'He's always been such a wonderful help and now he feels as if he's a burden.'

'You must let me know if I can help,' Nell said.

'Well, that's exactly why I need to talk to you, dear.

Come on in.' Jean stepped aside to let them enter. 'Sam's having a nap, but come and take a peek at him.'

As they followed Jean through to a back bedroom, Nell remembered the other time she'd seen Sam. She'd been expecting a replica of Tegan, had been on tenterhooks, ready for a mirror image of the baby she'd given up so many years ago.

But Tegan had been tiny and feminine, with a neat cap of soft, dark hair and tidy little features. Sam, by contrast, was chubby-cheeked and blond and his hands were plump and broad, making sturdy fists. He had been wearing a blue striped top like a miniature football jersey and he'd looked unmistakably masculine.

Now, as Nell stood with Jacob looking down at Sam in the old-fashioned, unpainted timber cot, she whispered, 'He's a bonny boy, isn't he?'

Jacob was standing very still, his gaze fixed on the sleeping baby.

Their grandson.

'He's *very* bonny,' he agreed at last. 'A real little bruiser.'

His voice sounded choked, but Nell heard unmistakable pride and when she looked up she was shocked to see the sheen of tears in his eyes.

On impulse, she reached for his hand and gave it a reassuring squeeze. His answering, shiny-eyed smile was so touching it sent tiny thrills flashing through her all the way to her toes.

'Sam looks like a lamb at the moment, but he isn't always as peaceful as this,' Jean warned them. 'There are times when he roars so loudly I swear he's a lion cub.'

They murmured their sympathy and tiptoed back to the front room. Bill was awake now and they were introduced.

He offered them a crooked left-handed smile but, in spite of his stroke, his eyes sparkled with good humour.

Jean dropped a quick kiss on his forehead and gave him an affectionate pat on the arm. 'Have you had morning tea?' she asked Nell and Jacob.

They assured her that they had and, as they sat, Jacob chose a spot on the sofa next to Nell.

Bill pointed to a photograph album on the coffee table and Jean picked it up quickly and handed it to them. 'We thought you'd like to see more photographs of Tegan.'

Nell knew straight away that it was going to be a battle to look at these snapshots of her daughter's life without getting tearful. Her hand shook as she turned the first page to a picture of the Brownes looking serious and middle-aged and almost frightened of their tiny newborn daughter, wrapped in a crocheted bonnet and lacy shawl.

Aware of Jacob sitting still as a rock beside her, she hardly dared to breathe as she turned more pages. Together they encountered pictures of Tegan as a small baby, as a grinning toddler, a lively little girl with her dark hair pulled into ponytails and predictable pink bows. Then there was Tegan in a striped swimsuit, her face covered in chocolate ice cream, in a school uniform, growing taller and missing teeth, frowning with concentration as she blew out birthday candles.

Nell felt her face begin to crumple.

We were never there for any of it, no part of our daughter's life.

She closed the book and took a deep breath.

'Tegan adored all the cards you sent for her birthdays and at Christmas, Nell,' said Jean.

Nell pressed her hands to her face. Any minute now she would be a mess.

Beside her, Jacob shifted uneasily. 'You said there was something you needed to discuss.' He spoke perhaps a little more loudly than he'd meant to.

Jean nodded. 'I'd like to explain our terrible dilemma.' She hesitated, as if she was sorting out in her mind what she needed to say. 'I'm Sam's guardian, you see. But we never dreamed that a young woman like Tegan could—' She had to stop and reach for a handkerchief, then dabbed at her eyes and blew her nose. 'Tegan was doing so well caring for the baby,' she said as she regained her composure. 'It never dawned on us that we would lose her and have to take responsibility for raising Sam.'

'It must be very hard,' Nell agreed.

'Especially at our age. Sam wakes several times during the night and now, with poor Bill's stroke, we have so many trips during the day for his medical appointments. You wouldn't believe how many people we have to see—doctors, physiotherapists, occupational therapists, speech pathologists.'

Jacob leaned forward, elbows on knees, his gaze intent. 'You really need help, don't you?'

'I'm afraid I do. I love little Sam, but Bill has to be my first priority now.' Jean patted her husband's arm and smiled fondly. 'The thing is, it's not just caring for Sam while he's a baby that I have to think about. There's the long-term, too. Raising him through childhood, through school and beyond.'

It was a daunting prospect. And Nell couldn't help thinking how stifling it would be for a lively little boy to grow up with an ageing grandmother and an invalid grandfather.

Jean lifted her hands in a gesture of helplessness. 'I feel torn in all directions, but I really don't see how we can be adequate parents for a growing boy. We were almost too old to adopt Tegan. And now—' She ran worried fingers through her thin hair.

'What are your options?' Jacob asked while Nell's heart began to thump as she guessed where this might be heading. Was Jean going to ask her to care for Sam on a permanent basis?

The thought awoke the hollow pain that had haunted her for many years after her parents had taken Tegan away. She'd eventually trained herself to put pregnancy and babies out of her mind, but now she felt stirrings of excitement, felt a leap of hope, like a rocket launching into a dark sky.

'I have two options,' Jean said. 'One is to hand over Sam to the state, but that certainly wouldn't be our preference. The other—'

Jean paused and Nell held her breath.

'I've had my solicitor check on the legalities of an alternative,' Jean said. 'And I can hand over my guardianship to a suitable person. It needs to be approved by a magistrate in a lower court, with the support of the child care authorities.'

By now Nell's heart was drumming so loudly she was sure everyone in the room must be able to hear it.

'Do you have someone in mind?' Jacob asked.

Every part of Nell tensed with anticipation.

Elbows on knees, Jacob leaned further forward. 'Have you considered Sam's father?'

Nell gasped. *Sam's father...* Good heavens, she hadn't given him a thought. Not a thought.

Who *was* Sam's father? Some scruffy teenager?

Good grief, already she was sounding as bad as *her* parents.

'We did quiz Tegan about Sam's father,' Jean said slowly, almost unwillingly. 'But she was a very determined, single-minded girl. So independent. She'd totally come to terms with being a single mother. When we pressed her, she said she would eventually let the father into their lives, but it would be very much on her terms.'

'But didn't she tell you his name?' Jacob persisted.

Jean shook her head. 'I got the impression that she might have regretted their encounter, that she didn't see him as long-term partner material.'

Jacob frowned. 'Hasn't anyone tried to trace him?'

'I'm afraid Tegan insisted on leaving his name off the birth certificate, so we have nothing to go on.' Jean glanced at her husband as if she wanted him to back her up, but he'd nodded off again.

Nell could understand that Jacob's sympathy would be with Sam's father, but she was selfishly glad that he wasn't in the picture.

The more she thought about taking care of little Sam, the more she loved the idea. She could easily imagine a baby in her life. She could picture herself giving him a bath, putting talcum powder and baby cream on him and dressing him in dear little clothes like the ones she'd bought as gifts for so many of her friends' babies.

It seemed very fitting for her to take care of Tegan's baby, almost as if the universe were making recompense for the baby she had lost. At night she could sit in her rocking-chair and cuddle Sam close. She'd give him his bottle and he would fall asleep in her arms while she rocked him.

'Our other problem is that Bill and I don't have any close relatives,' Jean was saying. 'Only older friends of our own age.' She gave a self-conscious little shrug of her thin shoulders. 'Poor little Sam doesn't want to be surrounded by a bunch of old crocks.'

The honesty of this silenced both Nell and Jacob.

Jean straightened her shoulders, looked resolute. 'It

might come as a shock, but I assure you we've talked this through at length. Bill and I want to raise the possibility of you, Nell, taking over as guardian.'

Here it was. Out in the open. Nell pressed a hand over her thumping heart. She turned to Jacob, but her joyous smile was frozen by the cheerlessness in his face.

Oh, help. How selfish she was. Sam was his grandson too. And he'd already missed out on knowing Tegan. But how could they share Sam? Jacob lived in Queensland.

Jean was watching them nervously, waiting for an answer.

'I feel very honoured that you would trust me with Sam,' Nell said. 'It's a big responsibility. A little life in my hands.'

'We'd trust you, Nell.'

'But—but you know so little about me.'

Jean's eyes widened. 'I feel as if I've known about you for a very long time.'

'Really?'

'I've been reading about your charity work in the papers for years now. And you've been sending Tegan birthday cards since she was five years old. I've sensed it's been an effort for you to keep your distance, but you let us get on with our lives and we really appreciated that.'

Nell was gratified that Jean had understood.

'And then there's been this past week, since the accident,' Jean said, as if she were throwing down a trump card. 'I've really got to know you well and you've been so very kind.'

Nell wondered what Jacob was thinking about this, but his face was more composed now and it was hard to tell. She turned back to Jean. 'I don't suppose there'd be any difficulty getting the magistrate's approval?'

'Oh, I don't think there'd be any problem there. My solicitor tells me you're so well-known in legal circles, there's any number of people willing to give you a glowing reference.'

'Looks like you have it in the bag, Nell,' Jacob said dryly.

'There would have to be a kind of trial period,' Jean warned. 'To test the waters, so to speak. It will take about a month, I'm told, before the legal aspects are sorted out and you could have full custody. But we could place Sam in your temporary care any time.'

Nell nodded thoughtfully. 'And when were you hoping that might happen?'

'Well, I assume you'd like a little time to think about it.'

'I don't really need time. I—I'm perfectly free to take care of Sam. And I'd love to.'

'Oh, Nell.' Jean's eyes shone with tears, but she looked exceptionally pleased. 'Oh, bless you. That's wonderful'

'So you just have to name a day.'

Jean blushed and clapped her hands to the sides of her reddened face. 'This must sound terrible, but would tomorrow be too soon?'

'I know what you're thinking,' Nell said later, as Jacob drove the Mercedes back to Williamstown.

'What am I thinking?'

'That Jean totally overlooked the possibility that you might like to care for Sam.'

He gave a shrug that was anything but casual. 'It's not at all surprising. Jean doesn't know me from Adam.'

'But you still feel that the rights of fathers are too often overlooked.'

'It's a universal truth, isn't it?'

'Unfortunately, yes.' Nell watched the suburban houses flash past, their pointed rooftops looking like rows of red-tiled teeth. 'It's very difficult, isn't it? We certainly wouldn't want to start a custody battle and, as the mother, I—'

'You're the *grandmother*, Nell,' Jacob corrected, with a wry quarter smile.

She rolled her eyes at him.

'The truth is,' he said, 'we both have a claim, but the Brownes don't know me. And we can't split the poor little fellow in two.'

'Of course we can't. And, if you were honest, you'd have to admit it would be very hard for you to take on a baby.'

'Not necessarily.'

'Think about it, Jacob. Imagine trying to care for a little baby on your Outback cattle property.'

'It happens all the time.'

'Oh, yes? And how many single dads do you know in the Outback?'

He shrugged. 'I admit I don't know any personally.'

'Because it would be next to impossible to run an enormous cattle property and look after a baby at the same time. You're probably picturing Sam as a little boy, riding horses, but think about what caring for a tiny baby entails. All the bottles and formula, the nappy-changing, the sleepless nights.'

'Whoa there.' Jacob lifted a hand from the steering wheel.

'But I'm making valid points.' This was so like a man, to skim over the nitty-gritty domestic details.

He smiled gently, almost sadly. 'Keep your hair on, Nell. I'm not going to try to take Sam away from you. I'm actually delighted that you're going to care for him. You'll be wonderful.'

She released her breath with a sigh, realised she had been getting unnecessarily worked up. The thing was,

Jacob might not be demanding his rights to Sam, but she knew he wasn't happy about being excluded again. What a sad, complicated state of affairs this was.

It was time to turn off the freeway and they let the subject drop until they reached her house. When they pulled up at her front gate, Jacob turned off the ignition but he remained in his seat, with one hand resting lightly on the steering wheel as he looked ahead through the windscreen at her neat suburban street.

Nell couldn't help admiring his profile—the high brow furrowed in thought, the strong nose, the attractive cleft in his chin. 'What are you thinking now?' she asked.

'About that photo album at the Brownes'. All those snapshots of Tegan's life. All those milestones.' His long tanned fingers tightened around the steering wheel. 'I was her father and I was never there. Not for one event, big or small, and neither were you, Nell. We were *never* a part of our daughter's life.'

Her throat was suddenly so choked she couldn't speak.

'I don't want a repeat of that with Sam.'

Eventually, she asked, 'What can we do?'

'I don't know,' he admitted grimly, but then he turned to her and the tiniest hint of warmth crept into his eyes. 'Let me sleep on it.'

'Sleep on it?'

'Bad idea?'

'Oh, in theory it's fine, I suppose. It's just that I haven't been sleeping very well lately.' She hadn't been able to sleep properly for days, not since she'd heard about Tegan's accident. Last night had been particularly bad. Seeing Jacob again had been enough to wreck her sleep, but now there was the excitement of Sam. It was like being pumped with mind-frying drugs.

Jacob got out and came around to her side of the car. As he opened her door, she wondered if he was going to kiss her again and her insides fluttered in anticipation. Heaven help her, she could still remember intimate details of how beautifully this man had made love to her.

'Here's a better idea,' he said when she was standing on the footpath. 'Why don't we talk about this over dinner tonight?'

'Dinner?' Nell repeated the word as if she'd never heard it before. The thought of dressing up and going out to a restaurant with Jacob Tucker messed with her head, stole her breath.

From the waterfront, a short block away, she heard the blast of a ferry's horn and the high-pitched screams of seagulls.

Jacob's eyes twinkled. 'You understand the concept of dinner, don't you? Two people go to a restaurant, sit at a table and enjoy a meal, usually an evening meal.'

She gave him a withering look. To go to dinner with him would feel like a date. A date with Jacob after twenty years…

'If you're going to take charge of the baby tomorrow, you should enjoy a night out,' he urged. 'Who knows what your life will be like after that? This might be your last night of freedom.'

'That's true.'

Smiling, Jacob ducked his head to catch the expression in her eyes. 'I'll take that as a yes, then?'

When he smiled at her like that there was no way she could refuse.

'I guess it's a yes.' Nell returned his smile shyly. 'Thank

you,' she added, almost as an afterthought. 'But just for dinner.' It was important to keep this simple. No complications. 'I don't want a late night.'

'How about an Italian place on Lygon Street?'

Lygon Street, made famous after the welcome influx of Italian immigrants, was one of Melbourne's best known restaurant precincts. She'd spent many a warm summer's evening there, enjoying the relaxing, friendly atmosphere and the wonderful food.

'Why not?' she said. 'Lygon Street would be perfect.'

CHAPTER FOUR

HANDS in pockets, head down, Jacob paced Melbourne's central business district, hurrying along Spencer Street, Collins, King and Bourke Streets with little sense of direction or purpose. He passed some of Australia's finest department stores, many wonderful bookshops and cafés, but paid them scant attention.

He'd never liked the big smoke, with its endless streams of traffic, its towering concrete buildings blocking the sky, its dank and smelly back streets. He always felt sorry for the blank-faced pedestrians, dressed in dark suits all year round, always hurrying, constantly bombarded by advertisements urging them to spend, spend, spend.

After a few days in Sydney or Melbourne, he was itching to be back in the bush, with wide open spaces, the big sky, the smell of gum leaves and clean sunshine. Even the dust stirred up by cattle was preferable to the exhaust fumes of city traffic.

He would give anything to be able to spirit Sam away from the city and he thought it was rather one-eyed of Nell to wave aside any suggestion that Sam could grow up in the Outback. She'd had a country childhood. She knew how good it could be.

Bush kids were fit and supremely capable. They learned to be self-reliant and to make their own fun outdoors, instead of sitting about, glued to television sets and video games. There was no better place for Sam to grow up.

But it wasn't going to happen. Jacob knew he couldn't stake a claim on the kid. Not now that he'd heard Nell's full story. Not now he'd spent a morning in her company, listening to her, watching her, discovering in the self-assured woman pleasing glimpses of the high-spirited girl he'd loved.

He had no doubt that Nell had earned this chance to be Sam's mother. But the looming distance between himself and Sam bothered him—*really* bothered him. Thousands of kilometres of separation. And once Nell had their grandson in her care, Jacob would only be able to visit him on her terms.

It wasn't, in any way, satisfactory.

Teeth gritted, brow fixed in a frown, he joined a group of pedestrians crossing Swanson Street at the lights and walked on.

At least Nell's husband wasn't in the picture. Jacob wasn't entirely sure how this made a difference, except that he'd kissed her on the strength of it…

And what wouldn't he have given to have let that kiss go on and on?

But that was fantasy. On the other hand, the issue of Sam's unnamed father was real. It was all very well for Jean Browne to act as if the father didn't exist, but there was a man out there, perhaps a young man of nineteen or twenty, who had a right to be consulted.

Fathers, and grandfathers for that matter, were important to boys. Jacob's own dad had died when he was very young and he'd missed the chance to get to know him. It had been damned hard for his mother to raise a boy on her own and Jacob had grown up with a deep-seated urge to be a husband and father, a tower of strength for his family.

But at just nineteen that dream had gone pear-shaped.

He continued, pacing all afternoon until serious-faced commuters began to bustle out of offices and on to trams and trains and it was time to head back to his hotel, to shower and change for dinner.

As he crossed the footbridge over the Yarra River to the South Bank, his disconnected thoughts suddenly fused and he made a decision. His plan of action would begin tonight.

Shortly before seven, Jacob walked up the path to Nell's front door. It was a beautiful evening and he took a deep lungful of air, laden with the scents of the sea and of lavender and roses. When Nell opened the door, however, he almost forgot to take another breath.

She was wearing a dark green dress with a ruffled top and a slim-fitting skirt and she'd threaded gold hoops in her ears. Her hair was swept up into one of those intriguing loose knots that looked as if they were on the verge of falling apart, so that a fellow had to keep watching, just in case.

There was something incredibly alluring and ultra-feminine about the soft fabric of her dress. The darkness of the forest-green made her hair more golden than ever, her skin smoother, her eyes brighter.

He wanted to gather her in to him, to hold her, to feel the softness of her skin against his, to taste her lush mouth again.

Too soon, he warned himself, but it was difficult to forget the eager way Nell had used to melt against him when they had been nineteen, the way she'd made him feel like a god.

The more time he spent with her, the more the memories flooded back, until it was hard to think about anything but lying with her in the sweet grass beside the river…undoing the buttons on her blouse.

'Have you had a busy afternoon?' she asked.

Jacob blinked, tried to rein in his thoughts by looking at her feet. She was wearing elegant sandals made from little gold chains and her toenails were painted an attractive berry colour. But what had she said? *A busy afternoon?*

'No, not exactly,' he managed. 'Have you?'

'Very busy.' Her smile broadened and he realised that she was glowing and bubbling with excitement. 'I've been shopping. It was so much fun. Come in and I'll show you. Actually, I need your help with something.'

As he followed her down the hall to a small room at the back of the house, he tried not to stare at her behind and the way her hips swayed in the neat green dress.

'I've put most of the things in here for the moment.'

Against the far wall, a single bed was piled with bags of disposable nappies, tiny infant clothes and a white wicker basket holding talcum powder, cotton wipes and tubes of baby cream.

'You didn't buy all these things this afternoon, did you?'

'I'm afraid I did.' Nell tried to look apologetic, but she couldn't hide her delight.

'That's quite a feat.'

'You have no idea how many gorgeous baby things there are. Look at this.' She picked up a pale blue garment that looked like a micro-sized boiler suit with rabbits embroidered on the front. Her eyes flashed brightly as she grinned at him. 'Have you ever seen anything so cute?'

'I don't suppose I have.' But he only gave the little suit a cursory glance before looking again into her lovely blue eyes.

Their gazes held.

And time seemed to stand still.

Nell's grin trembled and Jacob's throat constricted as the happy sparkle in her eyes changed to awareness. Breathtaking awareness. It was as if they were sharing the same memory, the same sensuous tug deep inside, the spectacular rush of mutual appreciation that they'd recognised and explored all those years ago.

It was over in a moment. Too quickly—way too quickly, Nell looked down and folded the tiny garment with extraordinary care.

Jacob scratched at his jaw. 'So what help do you need?'

'Oh, it's the cot.' She became businesslike at once, pointing to a room across the hall. 'I've assembled it in there, in my room, but I'm worried that I haven't got the wing-nuts tight enough. I'd hate the thing to collapse the minute I try to put Sam in it.'

The irony almost made Jacob smile. Right at this moment, there was nothing on this earth he wanted more than to follow Nell into her bedroom, but hell, he was getting sidetracked. This wasn't part of his plan.

'Aren't you jumping the gun?'

'What gun? What do you mean? I need to have everything ready.'

Ahead of him, she pushed open her bedroom door and he caught a glimpse of a king-size bed covered with an exquisite handmade quilt in shades of aqua, lavender and deep blue silk.

He stopped short of the doorway, averted his gaze from the bed. 'What's the rush to assemble the cot when we still haven't discussed what's happening with Sam?' Damn! That wasn't what he'd meant to say, but he couldn't go into that bedroom now.

Nell whirled around. 'I thought—I assumed—' Her eyes were round with worry. Her mouth opened and shut.

'Wasn't the plan to discuss Sam's future over dinner?'

She sagged against the door jamb. 'But I thought—'

She looked so disappointed that Jacob felt an urge to wave the whole matter aside, to say anything, do anything to make her smile again, to see her as happy as she'd been when she'd showed him the bunny suit.

But he curbed the urge. He had a plan and he didn't want to jeopardise it.

'Let's go to dinner,' he said gently. 'There'll be plenty of time to tighten wing-nuts tomorrow, before we pick up Sam.'

The restaurants of Lygon Street spilled out on to footpaths packed with crowded tables. Laughter and the happy chatter of diners filled the summer night.

Nell and Jacob, however, were shown to a table in a discreet alcove inside.

'I thought it would be easier for us to talk in here,' Jacob said, as soon as the waiter left them.

Nell nodded her agreement and wished she felt calmer about the impending conversation. Trying to share Sam was complicated, but that wasn't the only reason she was feeling tense.

There was the Jacob factor.

Jacob Tucker—gorgeous, passionate Jacob Tucker, the man who'd turned her world upside down—was back in her life.

In. Her. Life.

They'd gone beyond the chance meeting, beyond the chat to fill the gaps in the past twenty years, and now Jacob was adding an unnecessary extra step by taking her out to dinner. Any way Nell looked at that move, it felt like a date.

And how was she expected to stay calm about that? The very thought…the tiniest possibility that she and Jacob might…

No, she couldn't let herself think about any kind of relationship with him. She'd had her chance when she'd been nineteen. Now she had to concentrate on Sam, on her responsibilities as a grandmother.

In a bid to calm down, she paid attention to their surroundings, to the whitewashed walls and trailing plants, terracotta floor tiles and red and white checked tablecloths, stout candles in amber glass covers.

She picked up the menu and studied it carefully, paying meticulous attention to every ingredient in every dish and then instantly forgetting what she'd read.

'I can recommend the mussels,' Jacob said. 'And the beef is particularly good.'

'So you've been here often?' she asked, surprised.

'A couple of times.'

Over the top of her menu, their eyes met and he smiled. *Oh, help.* His smile was sexy and slow and lit up his grey eyes and she was awash with girlish shivers and flutters.

Get over it. Remember Sam. His future is a serious matter.

'Would you like some wine?' Jacob asked.

'Thank you,' she said. 'You choose something.'

'Do you have a preference?'

'I like white.'

It seemed to Nell that Jacob only had to raise an

eyebrow before the waiter was hurrying to serve them. He ordered the very best Semillon Blanc.

'You've changed,' she commented, remembering the raw country youth with his unassuming manner and shy smile.

'I haven't really.'

'You seem…worldlier now.'

Jacob shrugged, gave her an offhand smile. 'People don't change, Nell. I've moved on, that's all.'

Was he right about that? Nell had to admit that Jacob had always radiated an arresting born-to-rule quality, even when he'd been her father's lowly employee.

'You've done well, haven't you?' she said.

'Well enough.'

Her uneasiness gave way to intrigue. 'I read about your success a few years ago. How did you manage it, Jacob? You had to start from scratch with nothing more than a jackaroo's wage. And cattle properties are so expensive these days.'

'Don't you remember the strategy I planned?'

Nell found herself blushing. She and Jacob had had many long conversations on the river bank, but after twenty years she mostly remembered the lovemaking.

The waiter arrived with their wine and went through the ritual of removing the cork, offering the wine for tasting, then pouring.

After he left, Jacob raised his glass and smiled another of his melting-moment smiles. 'Here's to us and to the next twenty years.'

Gulp. What on earth did that mean? Nell wished her hand wasn't shaking as she lifted her glass to touch his. 'Here's to Sam,' she said softly. After all, it was because of Sam that they were here, wasn't it?

Jacob's response was a mere dip of his head.

Nell took a sip of wine to find it was crisp and dry and delicious.

She set her glass down. 'You didn't answer my question, Jacob. I'm still curious about your success. I remember your big dreams, but I was never sure how you were going to put them into practice.'

He gave her a considering look, as if he was weighing up the benefits of discussing his business with her. He took another sip of his wine, put it down and settled back in his chair.

'I got wise fast,' he said. 'I knew the banks weren't going to lend me much money, so I had to look at alternatives. I decided there was no point in trying to find cash to buy land when I knew that livestock brought the real returns.'

'So what did you do?'

'I bought the cattle and leased the land I needed.'

'And it worked?'

'Sure. City companies often lease their offices, so I looked for the best land leasing and agistment deals. I had to start small, of course, but whenever I had a chance to buy more stock I leased pastures in different parts of Queensland, so I got a good geographical spread.'

'That's clever. Thinking outside the box.'

He looked pleased that she'd recognised this.

'And it makes so much sense,' she said. 'Especially now, with climate change and the unpredictability of the seasons.' Absorbed by these ideas, Nell gave the stem of her wineglass a thoughtful twist. 'But that kind of farming would mean expensive trucking costs.'

'I solved that by buying my own trucks.'

'Good heavens. I thought those things cost the earth.'

'I got the first one for a song.' Relaxing with one elbow hooked over the back of his chair, he couldn't suppress a smile. 'I came across it one wet season, bogged in a black soil crossing on the Diamantina. The fellows who bogged it swam the cattle out, but they were going to abandon the truck. I made them a ridiculous offer.'

Nell laughed, imagining the scene—the squelchy black mud, the cattle in the river, the drivers' frustration. 'How did you get it out?'

'Mates with bulldozers. Only took them a matter of days to haul it from the river, but it took me six months to get the truck into working order.'

'Well, good for you.' She felt excited for him, and could imagine how satisfying his achievements must have felt.

Their entrées arrived—mussels in a Sicilian sauce for Nell and beef capaccio with lemon for Jacob.

She wondered when they were going to discuss Sam, but Jacob kept steering their conversation in other directions and she didn't object. But she hoped he wasn't waiting until she was relaxed with wine and good food before springing some kind of trap for her.

He encouraged her to tell him more about her quilt making, which she was happy enough to do. She could rabbit on for hours about textiles and colours and designs, but she didn't want to bore him.

Then he asked, 'Do you still like horse riding?'

Coming out of the blue, the question caught her off guard. 'I haven't ridden a horse in years,' she admitted.

But the seed had been sown in fertile ground and suddenly Nell was remembering her girlhood, when she'd thought there was nothing more fabulous than to set out on horseback in the early morning, over grass sparkling with dew, flying down the hill to the creek.

Nothing had been more exhilarating than the thrill of roaring along the river flats, losing her hat and not caring because the power of the beast beneath her was so magnificent.

'I've a beautiful bay mare at Koomalong,' Jacob said, watching her carefully. 'You'd love the country up there. We've had a good season. The creeks are running.'

'What is this, Jacob? An invitation?'

'Sure.'

'But I—' Nonplussed, she stared at him, while her heart galloped wildly.

The waiter arrived to collect their plates and Nell picked up her wineglass to take a sip, hoping it would calm her.

'You're inviting me to visit you at your place?' she clarified when they were alone again.

'You're planning a month to get to know Sam. Why not do that at Koomalong?'

Her mouth fell open. 'A month? You're asking me to stay for a whole month?'

'You'd enjoy it.'

'I—I—' She took another huge gulp of wine and tried to think straight. 'You're not serious, are you?'

'Why not?'

'You can't just drop out of the sky and into my life and say, Hey, come live with me, as if the past twenty years haven't happened.'

'I realise that.'

'What are you saying, then?'

His smile did wicked things to Nell's stomach. 'I'm saying that we're grandparents of a baby boy who needs us. We're both very keen to be a significant part of his life and it's damned difficult to do that if we're living thousands of kilometres apart. So my invitation makes good sense.'

Nell couldn't *think* what to say. How could Jacob make such a crazy suggestion sound logical and practical?

Their main courses arrived—fettuccini for both of them—and she paid careful attention to her food, purposely avoiding his eyes.

He topped up her wineglass. 'Think about it, Nell.'

'Believe me, I'm thinking. But my brain's stuck in a groove.' She twirled ribbons of pasta around her fork and ate them before she went on. 'I'm stunned that you can treat this as if it's nothing more than a simple child-minding arrangement.'

'But it doesn't have to be complicated.'

She stared at Jacob. How could suddenly deciding to live together for a whole month after all this time be anything but complicated?

His grey eyes held hers and he smiled and, in spite of her bewilderment, she felt a delicious warmth spreading through her—warmth that had nothing to do with the wine.

She tried to concentrate on her food, but she was suddenly remembering another time when Jacob had simplified a very difficult and complicated situation—on the morning she'd told him she was pregnant.

Will you marry, me, Nell? I'll look after you, I promise. We'll be all right.

If her pig-headed father hadn't intervened she would have been able to marry Jacob then, to raise Tegan, to be that happy little family they'd dreamed of. She shivered, then gave a shake to dismiss it.

How amazing to think that now, twenty years later, there

was another baby and Jacob was making another proposal. Making it sound so simple, so possible…

Part of her longed to mindlessly accept, to plunge in. After all, that was how everything had begun. She and Jacob had plunged into the river when the branch had broken and he'd kissed her as they'd scrambled up the bank.

'It's not such a crazy idea, is it?'

His voice snapped her out of her reverie.

Embarrassed that he'd caught her smiling dreamily, she became prickly. 'We—we hardly know each other now. We can't go back to the past and expect to take up from where we were at nineteen.' She hardly recognised herself as being the same person she had been back then. 'You know next to nothing about me now.'

'I know enough,' he said very quietly. 'I know you love the bush and I know you're a free agent.'

'But you're totally overlooking how I *feel*.'

A muscle worked in his jaw. 'That's true.' His eyes lost their amused sparkle.

She realised he was waiting for her to go on, to tell him exactly how she felt, to tell him that his proposal was audacious and impossible. There was no way she could live with him because…

Because…

To Nell's dismay, her mind wouldn't supply an end to that sentence. She gave a frantic shake of her head. 'Right now, I feel very, *very* confused.'

To her dismay, Jacob seemed satisfied with that.

Unsettled by the happy light in his eyes, she said, 'I have commitments here. Customers.'

'You can deal with them over the Internet.'

'How do you know that?'

'I found your website just before I came out tonight. It's very efficient.' He pressed his point home. 'Emotions aside, if you look at this practically, you could bundle up your quilting things and take them anywhere.'

She blinked. Jacob thought he had this all worked out, as if she were an object to be moved as easily as his cattle. But what he very carefully wasn't saying was that they would be alone together. There might be a baby in the picture, but they would be a couple living together and, even though she was a supposedly mature woman of almost forty, she didn't think she was ready to ask him what, exactly, that implied.

She chose a more oblique angle. 'You can't just look at this as if it's part of your business plan, Jacob. Another brilliant stroke of lateral thinking.'

But he wasn't listening, Nell realised. He was staring at some people who'd just come into the restaurant. They were behind her and she didn't like to turn around.

'What's the matter?' she asked. Jacob was frowning ferociously.

He didn't reply, but the newcomers were passing their table now, a well-dressed couple, the man in an impeccable suit—

Nell almost choked on her drink as she recognised the neatly bearded figure of Robert Ruthven, accompanied by a young woman in a very fetching red dress. A blonde, like Nell, but at least ten years younger.

They sat two tables away.

'Is that who I think it is?' Jacob hissed.

'Yes, it's my ex,' Nell admitted faintly. 'How did you know?'

'I've seen photos of him. My mother keeps an eagle eye on all the social pages.'

Nell wished she didn't feel so rattled. It wasn't as if this was the first time she'd seen Robert since the divorce. But she felt uncomfortable to be caught here with Jacob. If she'd been dining with a neighbour or a girlfriend, she might have remained quite calm. But Jacob was the man who'd taken residence in their marriage like an uninvited ghost. Worse, he'd just invited her to go off with him into the Outback.

'Nell!' Jacob's hand reached across the table for hers. 'Are you OK?'

As he watched her, Jacob's heart was tearing itself into shreds. He wanted to protect Nell, to rush her away, to save her from this embarrassment.

'It's OK, Jacob. I'm fine.' Nell had taken several deep breaths and was back in control, which was just as well, because at that moment Robert looked in their direction.

At first he looked shocked, but then, with the practised skill of an experienced barrister, he smiled, said something to his companion and stood.

'Well, well,' he boomed sonorously as he strolled towards them. 'Fancy seeing you here, Nell.'

'Hello, Robert.' She managed to smile very brightly as she held out her hand.

Jacob was on his feet and she said, 'You must meet an old friend of mine, Jacob Tucker.'

Until that moment, when the two men shook hands, she hadn't realised how much taller and more powerfully built Jacob was.

'Jacob Tucker.' Robert offered him a smile through gritted teeth. 'Of course, I've heard of you.'

'Likewise,' said Jacob grimly.

Robert sent Nell an eloquent roll of his eyes and there

was no missing his message. *So this is the man you could never forget?*

A split second later, he was once again the smooth barrister. 'You have good taste, Mr Tucker.' For a moment he left the ambiguous comment up in the air, but when Nell and Jacob looked suitably puzzled, he smiled. 'The food here is excellent.'

He turned back to his companion, indicating to her to come over. 'You must meet Gabriella.'

Nell was certain that Robert puffed out his chest.

As she rose to meet the other woman, she noted with mild surprise that she didn't have any pangs of jealousy. She could smile at Robert's new girlfriend and wish her well without a qualm—with a marked sense of relief, actually.

Gabriella seemed quite nice, but rather shy, and the introductions were brief. Robert turned to Jacob and said with a hint of condescension, 'So you're down from the bush to kick up your heels in the bright lights?'

'Actually, I came to Melbourne to attend a funeral.' Jacob spoke quietly, but with a hint of challenge. 'And to deal with personal business.'

'Ah.' Robert took a step back. 'Nice to have met you. Enjoy your meal, Nell.' He looked, momentarily, as if he would have liked to keep on going, backing right out of the restaurant.

Seated again, Jacob said to Nell, 'Would you be happy to leave now, without dessert or coffee?'

'Yes, please. I've had plenty to eat.'

As he attended to the bill, she remembered that they hadn't finished their discussion about Sam. What would happen now?

On the footpath, Jacob said, 'We're going in opposite directions, so it makes sense to take separate taxis.'

So this was the end of the evening? 'You realise we haven't settled anything about Sam?' she said, feeling way too up in the air.

'I think we've made enough progress for one night.'

Had they? Jacob was being enigmatic when Nell wanted a black and white decision. She didn't want to admit it, but Robert's arrival had driven everything askew. It was so strange. She'd known every intimate thing about Robert—that he meticulously squeezed toothpaste tubes from the bottom up, that he liked to cut the corners off his toast and eat them first, that he always slept on his back with his mouth open.

She knew none of those things about Jacob and yet they'd been parents, were now grandparents. And Jacob stirred her in ways Robert never had.

The laughter of carefree diners floated around them as they walked back along the footpath to the taxi rank. The feeling that her discussion with Jacob hadn't finished properly, hadn't solved anything, bothered Nell, but there was a cab waiting. Jacob ushered her forward. 'You grab this one.'

The evening was over.

'What about Sam?' she said in sudden panic.

'I'll come with you to the Brownes' tomorrow. We've plenty of time to work everything out.'

'So we're going to sleep on this decision after all?'

An elusive emotion flickered in Jacob's eyes. 'I think you know how this will pan out, Nell.'

Her heart leapt. What did he mean? She searched his face and saw a tenderness that set a thousand yearnings stirring inside her, spreading wings.

Oh, Jacob, don't look at me like that. I can't risk breaking my heart over you again. I would never survive.

But she said, 'You're probably right. Things often make better sense in the morning. Thanks again for a lovely dinner.'

She got into the taxi and Jacob closed her door.

Automatically, she lifted her hand to wave, but touched the window instead. Jacob tapped the outside glass where her fingers touched and the not-quite contact sent tendrils of warmth up her arms.

He smiled at her as the vehicle took off and she could see him standing on the edge of the footpath with his hands shoved deep in his pockets. Overhead lights caught the sheen on his dark hair, but she thought he looked very lonely as he watched her, as he waited until she turned the corner and was out of sight.

CHAPTER FIVE

I LET that turkey of a husband spoil our night.

Jacob entered his hotel room and let out a long, deep sigh into its darkened interior. He'd taken one look at that smooth barrister, that expensively dressed, silver-tongued ex-husband of Nell's, and his careful plans had flown out of the window.

But, in all honesty, he had to admit that the encounter had upset him more than it had seemed to bother Nell.

He showered, turning the taps on hard in an attempt to wash the tension from his body. Afterwards, he helped himself to whisky from the mini-bar in his room, tossing the fiery spirits down in two gulps.

In a final bid to get Robert Ruthven from his thoughts, he crossed to his suitcase and carefully retrieved an envelope from an inside pocket. Then he flopped back on to the huge hotel bed, reached above and snapped on the reading light. He opened a letter written in a round, girlish hand on sky-blue stationery trimmed with white and yellow daisies.

Lying in the pool of golden light, he read the words that he already knew by heart.

Dear Mr Tucker,
My name is Tegan Browne. I am nineteen years old and, shortly after my birth, I was adopted by the

Browne family. My birth mother is Nell Ruthven, née Harrington, and I was recently given your name and told that you are my father.

I have no idea how you felt when I was given away. For years I was angry with both you and Nell, but now I'm nineteen I think I understand that decisions like adoption are complicated. I realise you might not even know I exist, so I'm sorry if this letter is a total shock, but I've decided I need to know more about you.

So here goes...

Hi, Dad.

Picture me smiling shyly as I say that, because it's weird to say hello after all this time, isn't it?

On the night I was told your name, I couldn't sleep. I kept saying your name over and over in my head...Jacob Tucker, Jacob Tucker, Jacob Tucker...

I could have been Tegan Tucker.

You have no idea how often I've tried to guess what you're like. When I was a kid, I looked at men on the train and wondered if one of them was you. Sometimes I'd choose a nice-looking guy and pretend he was my real father. But don't get me wrong, it's not because I've been neglected or anything. Bill and Jean Browne have been wonderful parents.

I searched for you on the Internet and I read that you're a bachelor still, which is none of my business, I guess, but it made me kind of sad. I could only find one photo of you on a website about cattle. You were on a horse and your face was mostly shaded by a big Akubra hat, but you looked really great.

You're a cattleman. Like wow! How cool is that? And you live in Outback Queensland. I guess you ride horses and catch wild bulls and walk like a cowboy. I think that's awesome.

I know our shared DNA might mean little to you, but I thought I'd tell you a few details about me. I'm 167 cm tall and I have dark hair and blue eyes and I'm divinely beautiful (joke). I'm no great scholar, but at school I loved art and music. I used to think about training to be an art teacher, but I took a year off when I finished school and I kind of bummed around and now, well, something's come up and I don't know what the future holds.

I like messing about in Jean's kitchen and I'm turning into a pretty starry cook. You should try my blueberry pancakes.

Anyway, I've rattled on for long enough for a first letter. I hope you write back. I would truly love to meet you.

Your very curious daughter,

Tegan

PS I think Jacob is a very nice name. It's on my list of favourite boys' names. And I have some other important news, which I'll tell you if you write back.

Jacob set the letter on the bedside table, switched off the reading lamp and lay in the darkness on top of the bedspread. He hadn't drawn the curtains so there was still a faint glow from the city lights outside and he could see red and blue flashes from a neon sign reflected on the ceiling.

Tegan's words played through his head.

Picture me smiling shyly…

…I read that you're a bachelor still, which is none of my business, I guess, but it made me kind of sad.

The colours on the ceiling blurred and he was forced to swipe at his eyes with the backs of his hands, but the damn tears wouldn't stop. He'd read Tegan's letter a thousand times and it always tore at his heart. The openness of her communication, the youthful informality choked him up every time.

His little girl. The precious baby he'd made with Nell.

Her letter, like the photos he'd seen at the Brownes' today, was such a brief, tantalising glimpse into his daughter's personality, her life.

Jacob rolled onto his side and let out a painful sigh. Tegan hadn't mentioned her pregnancy, but he was pretty certain that the extra news she had been going to tell him was about the baby. If there had been another letter, would she have given him the name of her child's father?

What about that guy? It didn't seem possible that Tegan could write such a touching letter to her birth father and yet ignore the rights of her own baby's father.

Who was that young man? Where was he now?

It was something Jacob had to find out, no matter what happened tomorrow when he went with Nell to collect Sam.

Lying with his hands folded beneath his head, he found himself thinking about his own father and the photo that he kept hidden away in an old album.

His father hadn't been a cattleman, but he had loved the Outback and loved to ride horses and in the photo Jacob, aged two, was up in the saddle in front of him.

As a boy, Jacob had stared at that photo so often it was imprinted on his brain. That unfamiliar masculine figure on horseback had been his hero.

He could see the image now, could see his dad in a wide-brimmed hat that shaded his dark eyes, his straight nose and smiling mouth. His cotton shirt sleeves were rolled up, revealing strong, sinewy forearms. His hands were suntanned and long-fingered, one loosely holding the reins, the other curved protectively to hold the dark-haired little boy against him.

There were times when Jacob was sure he could remember that photo being taken, could remember that strong arm holding him close, could feel the texture of the rough cotton shirt against his back, the smoothness of the leather saddle beneath him.

He thought about Sam and felt an unbearable longing to have the boy in his life.

Tomorrow…

Jacob let out a soft groan. Had he ruined his chances?

He'd handled this evening so badly. He'd allowed Nell's ex to spoil their dinner and then he'd felt compelled to let the whole matter of Koomalong drop. Which meant he was no closer to his goal, and that was crazy.

Tomorrow was his last chance.

Nell dreamed of making love with Jacob, but she woke to a grim dawn, an empty bed and rain lashing against her bedroom window. She lay very still, enveloped by an overwhelming longing for her dream to continue, for Jacob's lips on hers, his arms about her, his body covering her.

Closing her eyes, she wished she could stay in the past. She wanted to be that reckless, careless girl again, longed for that time when her life had been focused on a single track, when her summer had been defined by her secret trysts with Jacob Tucker.

How resourceful she'd been back then, finding a sheltered glade inside a grove of trees on the river bank for their 'second date', sending a carefully coded message to Jacob via his mother, their innocent go-between.

She'd relished the danger and the secrecy.

'You know your father will sack me if he finds us,' Jacob said when he met her that second time. 'He warned me you were coming home, said there'd be hell to pay if I went anywhere near you.'

'Would you rather not come here, then?' she asked, disappointed.

He smiled shyly, pulled her in for a kiss. 'I don't think I can stay away.'

'That's settled, then.' She tried to sound calm but inside she was doing cartwheels. Already she was mad about Jacob. 'We should be OK at this time of the morning. My parents like to sleep in.'

'Yeah. Your father's the only cattleman I've worked for who isn't up with the birds.'

It was well-known in the district that her father was lazy, but Nell didn't want to waste time talking about him. She and Jacob sat together on a shaded patch of grass, their backs against the broad base of a gum-tree. 'It's your turn today,' she said. 'You have to tell me all about yourself.'

He grinned. 'I bet my mum's already told you everything you need to know about me.'

'Maggie's very proud of you,' Nell agreed. 'But in a nice way. She's not boastful, although I can tell she really loves you.' After a bit, she said, 'I've been wondering about your father.'

Good grief, she'd been blunt in those days.

Jacob's smile faded. 'My father died when I was two.'

'I'm sorry.' Nell could instantly tell how much this hurt him. 'That's so sad, Jacob. Do you mind—can I ask what happened?'

He shrugged. 'He was an engineer with the Main Roads

and he was inspecting a work project on a road out near Longreach. There was motorist who didn't slow down.'

Jacob's eyes grew dark and she could see that his father's death had left an enormous hole in his life. Nell gave him a hug.

Jacob repaid her with a kiss. Cupping her face in his hands, he kissed her sweetly, tenderly, making her insides swoop and drop, as if she were riding on a Ferris wheel.

'What else do you want to know about me?' he prompted, as he continued to hold her close.

'Um—' Nell's head was still spinning. *Where did you learn to kiss like that?* 'Um—have you always lived in the Outback?'

'Pretty much. Mum and I have lived all over the place—Western Australia, the Northern Territory, Queensland.'

'And I suppose you've had lots of girlfriends?'

His face broke into a slow smile. 'None you need to worry about.' He cocked his head to one side and his eyes were breathtakingly serious as he sifted strands of her hair through his fingers. 'You're beautiful, Nell. I bet you've had hundreds of guys chasing you in Brisbane.'

'Hardly hundreds. And no one as nice as you.'

She was rewarded with another kiss and it wasn't nearly as gentle as the first. The intensity of it stole her breath, thrilled her, sent her blood racing. She'd swear she'd never been kissed with so much passion.

'About those college parties you were telling me about,' Jacob murmured huskily, close to her ear. 'What happens after the eight minutes of chit-chat?'

'Um—' Nell struggled to breathe normally. 'If people decide to hook up, it's—it's up to them what happens next.'

He wound a strand of her hair around his finger. 'If we

were in the city, I guess I'd take you to the movies or to dinner or something.'

'Or something.'

He smiled again and his eyes revealed an unguarded warmth and emotion that sent Nell's heart thrumming. She longed for him to start kissing her again, knowing they were both burning up.

'No chance of movies or dinner for us.' His voice sounded hoarse.

'Then I guess that leaves us with *or something*,' she said bravely.

His smile turned shaky and his fingertips traced an electrifying line from her hairline down the side of her face to the little hollow at the base of her throat. Nell was on fire, almost bursting out of her skin.

Please keep touching me—please.

His fingers moved to the V at the neck of her blouse, and then to her first button, and Nell was drowning in a haze of heat. She willed him to undo that button, to undo all of them. She'd never offered herself to any man, but now she could think of nothing but how much she wanted Jacob, wanted his hands to touch her, to caress her intimately.

Looking back now, twenty years later, Nell was still amazed by the force of her youthful impatience. She could remember the way she'd thrown her arms about Jacob's neck, had kissed him hard, arching into him so that he could have no doubt what she wanted. And, in response, he'd attended to every one of her buttons and they'd made love.

She supposed that first time must have been more about passion than finesse, but she could only remember how blissfully happy she'd been.

There had only been one problem. They'd both been so carried away with the heady excitement of discovering each other that they hadn't waited till Jacob made a trip to the pharmacy in Roma.

'Morning, Nell.'

Nell was putting out the rubbish when her neighbour's cheery face popped over the fence.

Rosie O'Donnell was grinning at her from beneath an unruly mop of brown curls. 'I'm guessing you must be on top of the world.'

Nell tried not to look too surprised. 'Why would you think that?'

Rosie rolled her eyes to the pale morning sky. 'I've seen your visitor. Man, oh, man, Nell. Have you struck the jackpot, or what?'

'Which visitor?' Nell asked, playing dumb, as if she couldn't guess who'd put that silly grin on Rosie's face.

'Who else but the six foot plus, deadly handsome guy who's been calling on you?'

Nell dismissed this with an airy wave. 'Oh, that's just Jacob. He's an old friend from way back.'

'Old friend, huh? Every woman should be so lucky.'

'We were both at a funeral,' Nell added, hoping to dampen her neighbour's unwelcome enthusiasm.

Rosie simply shrugged.

And Nell tried to look just as nonchalant. She knew the subject of her going to Koomalong would resurface today, but her feelings about it were as confused as ever.

Rosie's eyes narrowed as if she sensed Nell's troubled thoughts. 'These blasts from the past can be unsettling, can't they?'

'Sometimes,' Nell agreed, and then, because she wanted to deflect the conversation right away from Jacob Tucker, she added, 'I'm going to have another man in my life.'

'Well, you don't muck about.'

'This fellow's seven weeks old.'

There was a second's puzzled silence before Rosie shrieked, 'A baby!'

Behind her back, Nell crossed her fingers as she stretched the truth. 'I'm adopting a baby boy.'

'But that's fantastic, Nell. It's wonderful.'

'I'm probably going to need loads of advice, Rosie.' Nell had helped out with friends' babies, but she couldn't remember the last time she'd changed a nappy. Rosie, as the mother of three boisterous little boys, had to be an expert.

'Oh, honey, it's always a little scary when you first bring a tiny baby home, but you can count on me. I'd love to help and the timing's perfect as far as I'm concerned. I've been hopelessly clucky lately, but Fred won't consider another mouth to feed.'

'You'll have to come and cuddle Sam then.'

'I'd adore to. Sing out any time you want a hand.'

'You can count on it.'

'So—everything's fine, son?'

Jacob's phone rang just as he was finishing his morning coffee in a café on the South Bank.

'Really fine,' he told his mother.

'And the—funeral went—well?'

'Actually, yes. I'm glad I came down here for it.'

'That's a relief.'

Given that Maggie had urged him to attend Tegan's funeral, this reaction was puzzling.

'I don't suppose you knew anyone there?'

Ahhh…now his dear mother was fishing, and almost certainly she was angling for news of Nell.

Casting a hasty glance at the diners breakfasting nearby, Jacob rose. 'Hang on a sec.' He set money to cover breakfast and a generous tip beside his coffee cup, strode out of the café and on to the paved embankment beside the Yarra. 'Are you still there?'

'Yes,' his mother said eagerly and, before Jacob could utter another word, she asked, 'Did you see Nell?'

'I did.'

'And?'

'And she's well.'

'Jacob, for heaven's sake, you know you've got to tell me more than that.'

Yes. Jacob totally understood her need for details. His mother had suffered almost as much as he had when they had been forced to leave Half Moon two decades ago. But how did he begin to tell her about Nell without telling her about Sam? And once he began talking about Sam, how did he stop himself from telling her about his proposition that Nell should live with him at Koomalong, about the stalemate they'd reached?

There was no point in stirring her unnecessarily.

His mother, however, had her own questions. 'Did Nell tell you she's divorced, Jacob?'

He felt his jaw unhinge. 'Yes, she did. How long have you known that?'

'Not long,' she replied airily. And then her voice dropped. 'Be careful, son. It wouldn't be easy to walk away from Nell again.'

'I'm not a crazy kid any more. Don't start worrying about ancient history.'

Disheartening silence followed this and then his mother sighed into the phone. 'Don't—don't hope for too much. I couldn't bear to see you hurt like that again.'

'Not a chance.' Jacob watched a group of schoolboys laughing and joshing as they took the pedestrian bridge over the river. 'To start with, old Harrington's not likely to come after me with a shotgun.'

There was an annoyed huff on the other end of the line. 'You know I didn't mean that.'

'Don't worry, this is very low-key. Nell and I have talked. That's all. We had a lot to catch up on.'

'I dare say. So—when are you heading back to Koomalong?'

'Ah—soon. Possibly in the next day or so.'

There was silence on the other end. Jacob said, 'I'll call you as soon as I've settled everything here.'

'All right. But Jacob—'

'Yes?'

'Just remember that life moves on. It has to. You can't recapture the past.'

How could he *not* remember that the past was lost to him? It was emblazoned on his brain in flashing neon lights. 'I'll remember,' he said.

Nell was grateful that her neighbour was a comrade in arms, but when she went back to her kitchen her optimism took a dive. She washed up the cereal bowl and mug she'd used for breakfast and confusion returned to settle on her shoulders like a ghostly blackbird.

Ambrose came into the kitchen and rubbed his silky flanks against her legs.

'What should I do, Ambrose?' She felt only a little foolish that she voiced the question aloud. 'Would I be horribly selfish if I stayed here in Melbourne and kept the baby to ourselves?'

Ambrose's mouth yawned wide in a silent miaow.

Nell sighed and told herself she was being sensible rather than selfish. She and Jacob could never recapture their youth. Their attraction back then might have been a spontaneous combustion, but it had been fuelled by the thrill of forbidden love, of youthful longing and secret trysts.

How different now—a practical arrangement between grandparents to facilitate caring for a baby. Nothing could be less romantic. There would be disappointment all round.

Anyway, it was arrogant of Jacob to assume that she could move easily, as if it were simply a matter of packing up her fabrics and sewing machine and abandoning her house and her friends for a whole month. His suggestion was preposterous. Was he really imagining that they could resume a relationship?

Nell closed her eyes and gripped the edge of the sink as a wave of heat rolled through her.

Help. This was what worried her most, wasn't it?

Jacob had given her one tiny kiss and she'd practically gone into orbit. She was as susceptible to Jacob's sexiness now as she'd been at nineteen.

But what if his proposed experiment at Koomalong didn't work out? She would be devastated and she couldn't risk that kind of pain again. And Sam might suffer too. Tiny babies were sensitive to their environment.

But then she remembered Jacob's disappointment yesterday. His pain.

We were never a part of our daughter's life.

As if that thought was the cue, a knock sounded on her front door. Nell thought she might cry as she hurried to answer it.

Jacob looked like heaven in blue jeans. 'Morning, ma'am. I believe you have a cot with dodgy wing-nuts?'

Each time she saw him she felt like a giddy schoolgirl—thumping heart, fluttering stomach, legs without bones. She gripped the door handle as Jacob held a pair of pliers high, like a trophy.

He was cool and relaxed, his manner almost flippant, and she didn't understand why or how that was possible. Yesterday, he had delayed this task because he'd wanted to settle everything about Sam. Last night they'd settled nothing and had parted uneasily.

So what did this apparent relaxation mean? Was Jacob putting on a brave face, or was he having second thoughts about Koomalong? Maybe he'd decided he'd be happy for her to care for Sam here in Melbourne. And maybe she had avoidance issues, but these weren't questions she wanted to ask.

'Come on in,' she said with a gesture for him to follow her down the hall.

With the purposeful lack of curiosity of a hired tradesman, Jacob headed straight for the cot in her bedroom.

Arms folded over her stomach, Nell leant a shoulder against the door frame and watched as he gave the cot a businesslike test rattle, then proceeded to tighten the wing nuts with the pliers.

She couldn't help admiring the way he worked. His hands were quick and efficient and she had a grandstand view of his back, so she could see the outline of his muscles rippling beneath his thin T-shirt and the breathtaking fit of his jeans. She concentrated on the back of his head.

But that was no help. His hair was dark brown, with no sign of thinning, and she liked the way it had been cut, making a neat, straight line—so *masculine*—across the back of his suntanned neck.

The job was done in a minute flat.

Jacob straightened and his grey eyes twinkled. 'The little fellow should be safe in there now.'

'Thank you.' Nell moistened her dry lips with her tongue.

Jacob watched her, then flicked his gaze to something beyond her left shoulder. 'How will you transport Sam? Do you have one of those special baby carriers for the car?'

'Yes. I tried to fit it yesterday afternoon, but I'm not totally confident I got it right. I—I wonder if you'd mind checking that it's secure?'

He nodded. 'Lead the way.'

Again, his readiness to help without question puzzled Nell.

'We still haven't sorted out where Sam's going to live,' she said when Jacob pronounced the baby carrier safe and ready for action.

He gave a slow shrug. 'You'll need a day or two to get used to him here. Let's take it one step at a time.'

'Just remember I haven't promised anything about coming to Queensland.'

'I know.'

'Jean might be very upset if she thought you were planning to take Sam all the way up there.'

Jacob nodded thoughtfully.

'As it is, she's going to be upset, handing over Sam.'

'You're right.' He looked sober as he considered this, but then he shrugged again. 'We'll soon find out, won't we?'

Jean's response surprised them both.

'Why not?' she said.

Nell stammered. 'W-we th-thought Queensland would be too far away from you.'

'But Tegan was very excited when she learned that Jacob was a cattleman. She loved the country. She went fruit picking after she finished school and I don't think she wanted to come back to the city. She actually told me once that she wished Sam could grow up in the country.'

'Really?' Nell's voice sounded as shaky as she felt.

'Oh, yes, dear.' Jean looked from one to the other and smiled knowingly. 'I'm sure Tegan would have loved to know you two were looking after Sam together. I forgot to tell you, Jacob. Sam's full name is Samuel Jacob.'

Jacob looked as stunned as Nell felt.

'And do you know what I think?' Jean asked them.

'What?' they replied in unison.

'Sam's a very lucky little boy. There was always a chance that neither of you would be interested in him. But to have both of you so keen to love him and take care of him—' Her eyes filled with tears, but she was smiling.

'Nothing's decided about Queensland yet,' Nell felt compelled to explain.

'Well, please don't keep Sam in Melbourne on my account. I know Tegan would have loved him to live in the Outback.' As an afterthought, Jean said, 'But if you went to Jacob's property, you'd keep in touch, wouldn't you? And you'd come back to sort things out with the courts?'

'Absolutely,' Nell and Jacob said together.

Over the next half hour, while they drank tea, Jean told them about Sam's milk formula and sleep patterns, his weight gains and immunisations.

Not wanting to forget anything, Nell took careful notes. But eventually Jean ran out of information.

'I'm repeating myself,' she said when she told them about Sam's weight gains for the third time. 'I think I've said enough. It's probably best if we make the handover quick and simple,' she said bravely. 'I'm not sure I could handle a prolonged farewell.'

Nell couldn't believe how suddenly nervous she felt, as if she were about to audition for a part in a play and had only remembered at the last minute that she hadn't learned her lines. Her heart knocked painfully as Jean extracted the sleeping Sam from his cot. She held her breath as he was handed to her.

Oh, how soft and warm and cuddly he was.

'Thank you,' she whispered, tears falling unchecked as she kissed Jean. 'Thank you so much. I promise I'll take good care of him and I'll definitely keep in touch.'

'Yes, dear. Feel free to ring me any time.'

Nothing felt real as they left the house and stowed a sports bag of baby clothes and nappies into Nell's car, plus another filled with formula and sterilising solution and bottles. Then they settled Sam into the baby carrier in the back of the car.

'Will you drive?' she asked Jacob. 'I'd like to keep an eye on Sam.' It was only half the truth. She felt too shaky and excited to take control of a vehicle and she had to get this right. Sam was such a huge responsibility.

'Sure,' Jacob said, smiling and holding his hand out for the keys.

As she snapped her seat belt, she spoke over her shoulder. 'We're taking you home, Sam.'

CHAPTER SIX

HOME.

Jacob turned in the driver's seat and his gaze met Nell. The unresolved question hung in the air between them. Where should Sam's home be?

Her throat constricted. When they got back to her cottage, they would have to finish their discussion, find an answer.

She looked down at her hands while Jacob started the car and they headed off, down the street.

'At least he's a good sleeper,' he said as they turned the corner.

'So far, so good.'

Right now, Sam looked angelic as he lay in his baby carrier on the back seat, his fine blond hair gleaming softly in the sunlight that streamed through the rear window and his pink mouth pouting a bubble of milk.

But they had hardly left Thornbury before he squirmed and pulled a face that made him look ridiculously like a very wrinkled old man.

'Sam's looking unhappy,' Nell announced nervously. 'He's squirming and moving,'

'I should think he would want to move.' Jacob smiled wryly as he took off at a green light.

'But he's turning red.' Nell didn't want to be nervous, but she'd had next to no practical experience with babies. 'I think he's waking up.'

'He has to wake some time.'

'But he shouldn't be waking now, should he? I thought babies were supposed to sleep in cars. Isn't something about the motion supposed to make them sleepy?'

As she said this, a tiny squawk emitted from the back seat. Scant seconds later, it was followed by a much louder wail. Then a full-bodied squawk. And another.

Oh, help! Was Sam missing Jean already? What should she do? He looked so distressed and sounded so miserable.

Nell wondered if she should ask Jacob to stop the car. They shouldn't just drive on, callously letting the baby cry, should they? Twisting in her seat, she watched Sam's small hand waving above him like a distress signal. She reached back and tried to catch it with her little finger.

'There, there,' she crooned as his fingers brushed the tips of hers. She dropped her hand lower and he clasped her little finger in a tight tiny fist.

It was lovely to feel him clutching her, needing her. 'You're all right, little man, don't cry.' How relieved she would be if she could pacify him.

Sam's wails grew stronger and louder, his face redder. He let go of her finger and his hand stiffened, fingers outstretched, imploring.

'He can't be hungry,' she said. 'Jean was quite certain that he doesn't need a feed for another hour or more.'

'Maybe it's wind,' Jacob suggested matter-of-factly.

How did he know about such things?

'Perhaps we'd better stop and see what the problem is.' Nell cast a doubtful eye over the busy lanes of traffic.

Jacob lifted his voice over Sam's cries. 'The Botanic Gardens aren't far away. How about I head over there? At least it will get us out of this traffic.'

'Yes!' Nell nodded gratefully. 'That's a good idea.'

Sam cries were ear-splitting by the time they pulled into the car park at the Royal Botanic Gardens. People getting into a car nearby turned to stare at them.

Nell flew out of her seat and fumbled with the straps binding Sam into his carrier. 'What's the matter, little man?'

Lifting him up, she felt his little body go rigid in her arms. It was like trying to cuddle a brick—a screaming brick. Nell tucked a muslin wrap around him and joggled him gently against her shoulder. She patted his back and when he didn't calm down she felt a shaft of real panic. She knew babies cried but she'd never heard one as upset as this.

What was wrong with him? He'd been fed, his nappy was dry. He couldn't have developed a dreadful disease in the short time since they'd left the Brownes'.

What if she couldn't calm him?

Jacob joined her and she shot him a frantic glance. He smiled, but she knew he must be thinking that her mothering skills were sub-zero.

'Why don't we take him for a walk?' he suggested.

'A walk? When he's screaming? Do you think it would help?'

'It's worth a try. You never know, it might soothe him.'

Nell directed a doubtful glare at the sweeping lawns, the majestic elms and oaks and the path circling the ornamental lake. The early morning rain had finished soon after breakfast and it was a lovely summer's day. Melburnians were out in force, enjoying their favourite parkland—joggers and parents pushing prams, toddlers entranced by the teeming birdlife—lots of babies, lots of small children. Only Sam was screaming.

Jacob didn't seem perturbed by the baby's uproar. He threw a protective arm around Nell's shoulders and she felt absurdly grateful for his reassuring presence. He clicked the remote control to lock the car doors and they began to walk, their footsteps in time as they crossed the gravelled car park to the path.

Sam kept yelling, but Jacob talked anyway.

'These gardens are my favourite part of Melbourne,' he said as the path led them down the slope towards the water.

'Let me guess—because it's full of trees and wide open spaces?'

'Absolutely. Being here is the next best thing to being in the bush.'

It was a not so subtle reminder. 'But parks are supposed to be tranquil places. Sam's disturbing the peace.'

'He's a tiny baby, Nell.'

She sighed. 'I know.' She gave Sam's back a firmer pat and hitched him higher on her shoulder. Almost immediately, he let out a huge burp.

And stopped crying.

'Goodness.' Nell lifted him away from her, so that she could look at him. 'Was that the problem?'

In the sunlight, Sam's fine hair was lit with gold. His blue eyes were still shiny with tears trembling on the end of dark lashes. He was staring at her with a look that suggested he was almost as surprised as she was that he'd stopped crying. He was absolutely gorgeous!

Nell smiled at Jacob. 'You were right. But how did you know he had wind?'

Returning her smile, he shrugged. 'I must have an acute understanding of infants.'

She wasn't buying that. 'Or you made a lucky guess.'

Grinning widely now, he snapped his fingers. 'Sprung.'

Nell laughed. And then she was instantly sobered by the realisation that this was the first time she'd laughed in ages.

Ages.

She remembered how often she and Jacob had laughed all those summers ago.

As she settled Sam back against her shoulder and walked on, her confusion about the tall, handsome man beside her returned. Jacob was slipping into her life with astonishing ease, but so far his role was hard to define. He was so much more than an old friend, more than a good egg lending a helping hand. He was almost a partner.

But the bottom line was that Jacob was Sam's grandfather. That was the reason he was here, taking a stroll through the park with her. That was why he wanted her at Koomalong.

Sam's grandpa.

She looked again at the tall, dark, not-yet-forty guy in blue jeans and almost giggled.

'What's so funny?'

'I was thinking that the universe has a perverse sense of humour, turning us into grandparents before we're out of our thirties.'

The skin around his eyes creased as he grinned. 'Don't worry, Nell. You make a very cute granny.'

She looked away and pressed a kiss to the top of Sam's head. He was warm and relaxed as he cuddled against her now, growing heavier as he snuggled in like a baby koala. The walk was indeed soothing him.

They passed a beautiful bright garden of massed perennials.

Jacob asked, 'Are your parents still living at Half Moon?'

Surprised by the question, but thankful for the change of subject, she answered readily. 'No. Haven't you heard? They had to leave.'

'How do you mean? What happened?'

'Dad, being the stubborn so-and-so that he is, wouldn't listen to all the warnings about global warming and drought. He overstocked and overgrazed and virtually ran the property into the ground. Then he couldn't repay his debts, so the bank foreclosed.'

Jacob let out a low whistle.

'My parents have moved to Rockhampton,' Nell told him. 'Dad works in the cattle sale yards now.'

She was rather grateful that Jacob made no comment. Heaven knew, he had plenty of grievances against her father and there were many things he could have said about how the mighty had fallen, but he probably didn't want to hurt her feelings.

'I've often wondered about your mum,' she said. 'How is she? Is she still living with you?'

'No way.' Jacob chuckled. 'She's married to a grazier in the Kimberley.'

'Really?' It was too late to hide her surprise. 'Wow, Jacob! That's wonderful.'

'She's got a beautiful home, a guy who's crazy about her, an extended step-family who adore her and she's as happy as a possum up a gum-tree.'

'I'm so pleased for her. I really liked her.'

It was the truth. Nell had genuinely liked Maggie Tucker and not just because she was Jacob's mum. Maggie was a handsome, fun-loving woman and a terrific cook. There'd been a warmth and an earthiness about her that Nell had found particularly appealing and strangely comforting. She'd spent many happy hours in Maggie's kitchen, in spite of her parents' disapproval.

'Maggie's teaching me to cook,' she'd told them. She could still remember the joy of learning from Maggie how to make perfect blueberry pancakes and scrumptious gingerbread. As for the chocolate pannacotta—yum!

'Your mother deserves to be happy,' she said.

'Yeah.' A fond smile warmed Jacob's face. He looked down at Sam. 'Speaking of happy—'

'Has he gone to sleep again?'

'Out like a light.'

'What a good little man.'

Speaking of happy...

Nell had never looked happier.

As they turned and walked back towards the car park, Jacob suspected that looking at Nell was a health hazard. She had always been lovely, but this morning, in the sunlight, holding the baby wrapped in a gauzy shawl, she was more beautiful than any Madonna painted by the great masters and Jacob had the pulse rate to prove it.

Nell's face had taken on a special tenderness, a mysterious sweetness that almost brought him to his knees.

With Sam in her arms she looked fulfilled and completely happy. And, like his mother, Nell was a woman who had copped more than her share of hard knocks, and she deserved this happiness.

What right did he have to put extra pressure on her by demanding that she make the huge shift to Koomalong? Could he really expect Nell to give up her cottage and her comfortable life here in Williamstown? She'd decorated the house with such care and made it her own. It was conveniently close to shops and the sea front and to pretty parkland.

He'd convinced himself that Sam would be better off in the Outback, but he couldn't deny that a seaside suburb had a lot of appeal for a small boy.

Now, looking at the expression of contentment on Nell's face, Jacob realised he had to back right off.

If he'd learned anything about women, it was that timing was everything and, right now, Nell's attention was tuned one hundred per cent in to Sam.

There was no point in trying to tell her that he still wanted her, as badly as he had when he'd been nineteen. Walking with her was not enough. Talking with her, watching the play of emotions on her expressive face, watching her holding Sam, was not enough. He needed her in *his* arms, needed the taste of her lips, the smell of her skin, her touch.

But there was every chance he'd totally scare her off if he tried to tell her that.

They reached the car park and Jacob pressed the central locking device. The car's lights flashed and the doors clicked. He opened the back door for Nell.

Nell, however, didn't move. She remained standing very still with Sam in her arms while she looked back at the green sweep of gardens, at the trees and the lake. And then she turned her attention to the street beyond the car park, to the busy lanes of jostling, honking traffic. Her gaze lifted to the skyscrapers—all glinting glass, concrete and metal—looked above them to a plane streaking through grey, smoggy clouds.

'Tegan was right,' she said quietly.

Fine hairs lifted on the back of Jacob's neck. 'What about?' His question was hardly more than a whisper.

'He likes open spaces.'

She smiled at him and he held his breath.

'And I think Sam needs both of us,' she said. 'Let's take him home and then we must talk about Koomalong.'

CHAPTER SEVEN

I THINK Sam needs both of us.

Nell couldn't believe she'd actually said that. She'd been so cautious, but now it was out and she was sure Jacob couldn't believe it either. He was looking at her as if she'd grown a third eye.

'Let's get Sam home first,' she said quickly. 'Then we can talk about it.'

Jacob sprang to life, moving aside so she could settle the baby back in the carrier. Luckily, Sam fell asleep and he slept all the way back to Williamstown. Jacob didn't press Nell to talk, for which she was extremely grateful. The enormity of what she'd said was sinking in and she was starting to feel the aftershocks.

When they reached her cottage, Jacob became businesslike, carrying all Sam's things inside and stacking them in the back room.

'I think Sam needs a nappy change,' Nell said, feeling his damp rump.

Jacob's eyes twinkled with amusement. 'Will this be a first for you?'

'Of course not. I've changed oodles of nappies for friends' babies.'

'Great, then I can watch and see how it's done.'

Oh, good one, Nell. She was ridiculously nervous as she laid Sam on a fresh towel on the spare bed. Her hands were all thumbs as she unsnapped and lowered his pants and removed the nappy. It didn't help that Sam kicked his legs madly during the entire process, so that his little feet kept getting in the way.

'Hmm,' said Jacob, watching over her shoulder. 'Impressive family jewels.'

'All baby boys look like that.' Nell was annoyed with herself for being flustered. She thrust a packet of baby wipes at him. 'Here, you have a go.'

Jacob looked as if he'd swallowed a bug. 'What am I supposed to do?'

'Wipe over his nappy area with one of these.'

'Hey, I'm still learning. I'm happy to watch you. You're doing great. You're a genuine expert.'

She smiled at him sweetly. 'I've a better idea. Why don't you put the kettle on? We're going to have to heat up his next bottle.'

'OK.' Jacob was about to leave when he took a closer look at Sam. 'Nell, look. He has a birthmark just like yours.' He pointed to a tiny strawberry splash on Sam's ankle.

Nell gulped. After all this time, Jacob remembered the butterfly shaped mark on her hip.

'What about the kettle?' she said without daring to meet his eyes.

He accepted this task in good humour and headed for the kitchen, leaving her to fumble her way through changing Sam into a fresh set of clothes.

The subject of Koomalong was left until after Sam had been fed and carefully burped and put to bed in the little cot in Nell's bedroom. She decided to tackle it over lunch—tuna and mayonnaise sandwiches and cups of tea in the kitchen.

Nervously, she said, 'OK, I guess it's time to talk.'

'Whenever you're ready.'

His attempt at nonchalance didn't fool Nell. He was as uptight as she was.

She took a deep breath, then let it out noisily. 'The thing is, I agree that a cattle property is a great place for raising children, especially boys. But, more than that, I do understand how awful it would be for you to miss out on getting to know Sam.'

He nodded solemnly.

'But, to be honest, Jacob, saying that scares me. Half of me thinks it's a crazy idea.'

'But it would only be for a month to start with.'

'That's thirty days, Jacob.'

'What are you afraid of?'

'That you—'

'Yes?'

'That we—' The sudden amusement in his eyes made this conversation a hundred times harder. 'We can't expect to turn back the clock twenty years.'

'Is that a careful way of saying that you don't think we can resurrect our relationship?'

The kitchen grew suddenly hot and close. Nell wished she could fan her flaming cheeks. 'I—um—certainly don't think we should assume that a relationship would be the—um—likely outcome.'

Good grief. Were there lingering hints of regret in her voice? Had she ever sounded so flummoxed?

She tried again. 'It's going to be a very tricky situation.

After all this time, we've probably romanticised the way we think about each other.'

Jacob's eyebrows rose and something disturbing in his expression forced Nell to study the remains of her sandwich.

'In reality,' she continued bravely. 'We've probably changed too much. I know I've changed and I'm sure you have, Jacob. And we only ever knew each other for such a short time. There's every chance that trying to live with each other won't work. We might be really disappointed. It could be a disaster.'

'That's always on the cards.' He spoke with annoying equanimity.

'So it's important to remember that I'd only be coming to Koomalong on a trial basis,' she said.

'There's no question about that. All three of us will be on trial. After all, we don't want to commit ourselves at this stage, do we?'

To her dismay, Nell realised that wasn't quite what she'd wanted him to say.

'It would be foolish to commit ourselves,' she told him.

Jacob smiled in a way that was both serious and gentle and he reached out and touched her cheek 'You won't regret this, Nell. You know how much you love the bush.' He traced a line on her cheek, creating a burning trail with his fingertips.

Nell struggled to breathe. Already he was breaking the rules! But, heaven help her, she was so vulnerable. Her skin was burning beneath his fingers. This one tiny intimacy was enough to launch her out of her chair and into his arms.

'Yoo-hoo! Anybody home?'

Nell jumped so quickly her chair fell backwards, clattering noisily on to the kitchen tiles. She saw her neighbour, Rosie, peering through the flyscreen door.

'Hi, Rosie,' she called, wincing at how out of breath and dizzy she sounded.

Rosie grinned and waved at her. 'I didn't mean to startle you, Nell. I was hoping I could take a peek at the new man in your life.'

Early in the evening, after attending to business in the city, Jacob returned to Nell's. As he pulled up, he could hear Sam's high-pitched cries and they grew louder as Nell opened the door.

'He's been grizzling like this for the past hour,' she said, gently rocking the unhappy fellow. 'The only thing that will keep him quiet is if I walk about and carry him. The minute I try to sit down he complains. But Rosie said her three boys were the same for the first couple of months.'

She looked apologetic. 'I hope you're not hungry. I haven't been able to do a thing about dinner.'

Jacob shrugged. 'It's a lovely evening. Why don't we take Sam for a stroll along the waterfront?'

'But don't you want to eat?'

'We can buy something, eat it looking out over the water.'

She beamed at him. 'I'll be ready in a jiffy.'

It was a beautiful summer's twilight. The sky was an extravagant lilac and scents from the gardens in Nell's street drifted slowly in the still air, blending with the smack of salt from the bay. Nell carried Sam, buttoned up in his warm little rabbit suit, and Jacob lugged the bag of essential baby things and more than one set of front curtains twitched as they passed.

In the row of shops around the corner, they bought fish and chips wrapped in layers of butcher's paper, cans of lemon drink, a bag of fat purple grapes and a bar of chocolate.

They crossed the road at the lights and went through the parkland that rimmed the water till they found a spare picnic table right near the edge of the bay. A gentle breeze drifted in from the water and on the far side they could see the twinkling lights of Melbourne.

'Here, I'll take him,' Jacob offered. 'I can eat standing up.'

'I hope we're not spoiling him,' Nell said as she handed Sam over.

'You can't spoil them at this age, can you?'

'I don't know.'

'I'd rather eat standing up than sit in comfort while he bellows his lungs out.'

'That's how I feel, too.'

Nell tore off a corner of the paper, wrapped it around a piece of hot, crunchy fish and handed it to Jacob.

He bit into it and grinned. 'Nothing beats fish, fresh from the sea.'

'That's something you can't get in the Outback.'

'True,' he admitted. 'But then, only a select few can appreciate the hidden delights of life in the bush.'

'Because they're so hidden,' Nell said, but she smiled to show that it was her attempt at a joke. She looked at Sam, who was very peaceful now, with his head on Jacob's bulky shoulder, his eyes closed. 'Who do you think he looks like?'

Jacob twisted his neck, trying to examine him. 'I've no idea. He has your colouring.'

'Maybe he looks like his father. Tegan did.'

'Poor girl.'

'She was beautiful, Jacob.'

'Yes,' he said softly. 'She was.'

A seagull swooped low and stole a chip. Nell shooed it away before it could get another. 'I wonder what kind of boy Sam will grow into. Whether he'll be artistic or sporty or good at school.'

'He might be a philosopher.'

She laughed. 'He'll probably end up a cattleman.'

'Could do worse.' Jacob helped himself to another piece of fish.

Nell said, 'You seem to have a definite knack with babies. Sam looks like he's gone to sleep.'

'Are you sure?' Jacob turned to give Nell a better view of the baby's face.

'He looks sound asleep to me.'

'I might try sitting down, then.'

Sam snuffled and squirmed as Jacob lowered himself on to the long timber seat opposite Nell, but he quickly settled again, snuggling against Jacob's shoulder.

Nell thought how gorgeous the pair of them looked. She snapped the top of a drink can and handed it to Jacob. 'You'll need this after that salty fish.'

He took a long drink, set the can down thoughtfully and stared off into the distance.

'You're very pensive,' Nell said.

He continued to frown.

'Is something the matter?'

'I can't help wondering what would have happened if I'd stared your father down that day when he charged in on us.'

'But you did,' she cried, startled by the sudden turn of his thoughts. 'Don't you remember?'

'I was too upset to think straight.'

'I'll never forget that day. Dad was so angry his eyes were almost shaking in his head, but you more than stood your ground, Jacob. You pushed me to one side and started marching towards him like Achilles challenging Hector.'

'All I remember is that I didn't stand up to your old man the way I wanted to. I was afraid he would hurt you, or my mother.'

'You were as stubborn as he was,' Nell told him, smiling a little at the vivid memory. 'I was terrified you'd try to fight—that he might go into one of his violent tempers and shoot you. In the end, I was the one who told you to go. I ordered you away.'

'Did you really?'

'It seemed to take forever. You both just stood there, taking deep breaths and staring at each other.'

She shivered as she remembered the tension of it, the awful journey back to the homestead, the fearsome control of her father and her removal to Melbourne, how she'd cried for weeks.

'Don't think about it now, Jacob.'

'There's no point, is there?'

'None at all. It's ancient history. Here, try one of these grapes. They're so sweet and juicy.'

When they'd finished their meal, they threw the paper and empty cans into a rubbish bin and walked together back to her house.

'Perhaps I should take Sam now,' she said at her front gate. 'He might be less disturbed if we swap here, rather than inside with the lights and everything.'

They'd handed the baby to each other several times now, so Nell had no idea why, this time, it took so long and felt so incredibly intimate. Perhaps it was a matter of proximity.

Jacob didn't step away and neither did she. And her skin grew tight and her breathing faltered as they stood together in the dusky twilight. And then Jacob dipped his head and kissed her cheek. 'Night, Nell.'

'Would you like to come inside?' she found herself whispering.

'I'd love to.' He dropped a feather-soft kiss on her brow. 'But I'm not going to.'

Oh.

Her disappointment was silly. This was the first day of a month-long trial.

And she should be grateful that Jacob was much more cautious now than he had been when they were nineteen.

From the front seat of Jacob's Range Rover, Nell smiled when she saw a set of five-barred gates and a weathered timber signpost bearing the name Koomalong in dark green lettering.

Their vehicle rattled over the cattle grid.

'I'll get the gate,' she called, opening her door as soon as the vehicle came to a halt and jumping down, as eager as a child, home from boarding school.

She pushed the gate open and smiled again as she heard the musical squeak of its rusty hinge. Was there ever a gate in the Outback that didn't have squeaky hinges? She watched the dusty vehicle pass through, closed the gate and stood, looking about her, taking everything in.

Beyond the gate, a dirt track led up a gentle, brown-grassed slope and, on the brow of the hill, a magnificent old gum-tree stood clear against the blue blaze of the sky. The tree's solid trunk was silvery-white and its soft, grey-green leaves hung with a familiar tapering droop.

Nell sniffed at the air. The Outback smelled exactly as she remembered. She dragged in a deeper breath, absorbing with it the scents of dusty earth and cattle and the subtler notes of dry grass, of sunshine and eucalyptus.

She'd had occasional trips into the countryside during her marriage, but Robert had been uncomfortable away from the city so they'd never stayed long. Now, a kookaburra broke into laughter and a thrill of excitement rippled through her.

It was good to be back.

'Are you going to stand there all day?' Jacob called to her.

Turning, she saw the white flash of his teeth in his tanned face as he grinned back at her.

'Coming,' she called. And then, as she climbed back into her seat and pulled the door shut, she thought, *Jacob's right. This is my country. It's so good to be back in the bush.*

She turned to check Sam in his carrier on the back seat, happily cocooned between Jacob's dogs—a Labrador and a blue cattle dog which they'd collected from a boarding kennel in Roma.

There'd been an agitated few minutes when the dogs had first seen Sam and the tension had escalated when they'd located Ambrose in a cage in the back of the vehicle. But, after a quiet word from Jacob and a scratch behind the dogs' ears, they had settled down beautifully.

Now, as Jacob drove along bumpy tracks that crossed grassy paddocks dotted with cattle and gum-trees, Nell could make out the course of a creek marked by the wattle trees and melaleucas that lined its banks. Another burst of kookaburras' laughter sounded and, from the stretch of brown grassland, the piercing three-note call of a spur-winged plover.

She began to feel as if she'd come home.

Which was pretty silly, considering this wasn't exactly a homecoming. She had no actual right to feel so choked up and sentimental. She was moving into Jacob's home on a trial basis. Not the same thing at all.

Who knew if this experiment would work?

She wasn't sure what Jacob expected. He had reverted to being very practical and helpful. And Nell had been totally occupied with learning to cope with Sam while packing up. Any hint of romance had been dropped.

If the nineteen-year-old Nell had been told that she and Jacob Tucker could have spent so much time in each other's company without sharing so much as a kiss, she would never have believed it. Nell still found it hard to believe.

Secretly, she'd wondered if Jacob and she were complicit in a crazy mind game where they'd both pretended not to want each other. She had even indulged in the dangerous fantasy that once they got to Koomalong they would fall in love again and give up pretending. The horrible thing was, she knew deep down that if their experiment failed she would leave Koomalong broken-hearted.

So this was potentially dangerous territory and as the track turned a corner and a low, sprawling, white homestead became visible through a grove of shade trees, she had no idea what lay ahead.

The situation became crystal clear, however, the minute Jacob brought the vehicle to a halt at the bottom of the homestead's front steps and a figure uncurled with catlike grace from a cane chair on the veranda.

Nell swallowed her gasp of surprise as a young woman—a long-legged, green-eyed, Titian-haired girl in tight jeans and a low-necked blouse—sauntered confidently down the steps, her smile radiant as she waved at them.

'Who's that?' she asked Jacob.

He groaned. 'A girl from Roma.'

'A girlfriend?'

'No,' he said through gritted teeth. 'I met her once at a party.'

Nell's fingers trembled as she unfastened her seat belt and she chastised herself for not being prepared for something like this. Any woman with reasonable eyesight knew that Jacob was an attractive man. Chances were, he had quite a fan club and she would have to get used to it.

Slipping quickly out of the vehicle, she turned her attention to the dogs and to Sam, while behind her the young woman embraced Jacob with noisy enthusiasm.

The dogs, eager to be out of the car, bounded away clearly ecstatic to be free, darting about the garden, sniffing, lifting legs, exploring.

Nell unbuckled the straps that had held Sam safe, scooping him up. 'This is your new home, little man.'

He was delightfully drowsy and warm as she lifted him out. She kissed his soft, chubby cheek and cuddled him close, was overawed once more by how quickly and completely this darling little fellow had claimed her heart.

'Ooh, the baby!' the girl shrieked. 'Jacob's housekeeper has been telling me all about him. I've been dying to meet him. His name's Sam, isn't it?'

The redhead scurried around to Nell's side of the Range Rover. 'Hello.' She beamed at Nell and countless silver bangles tinkled as she offered her hand. 'I'm Katrina.'

Nell smiled carefully. 'Hello, Katrina. I'm Nell.'

Katrina pulled a face at Sam, screwing up her nose and pouting her bright lips. 'Aren't you the cutest button?' Straightening, she smiled more coyly at Nell, lifting a smooth eyebrow. 'You must be the baby's nanny.'

'Not exactly,' Nell said quietly and with necessary dignity. 'I'm his grandmother.'

Katrina giggled nervously and then she smacked a hand over her mouth. Clearly puzzled, she turned to Jacob, who had joined them, looking thunderous.

'So she's—' Katrina hooked a thumb towards Nell, her frown deepening. 'So if Nell's the baby's grandmother, then that must mean that you and she—' Looking flustered and red-faced, she shot another anxious glance Jacob's way and finished her sentence with a flap of her hand, setting the bangles jangling again.

'It was all a long time ago,' Nell said, taking pity on her. 'Water under the bridge.'

Jacob nodded, which she took to be approval. 'Come on inside,' he said. 'I'll show you around.'

'Just a minute. I need to fetch Sam's bag of tricks out of the car and I should rescue poor Ambrose from the back. Here, Jacob, you take Sam.'

Katrina watched with hawklike attention as Nell handed Sam to Jacob. Nell wondered if the other woman felt the same little swooning sensation she always felt when she saw tiny Sam cradled in Jacob's big, muscular arms.

With the nappy bag in one hand and Ambrose's cage in the other, she followed Jacob and Katrina up the steps, across the deep veranda and into his house.

It was a lovely house, quite old in the traditional Queenslander style, with a ripple iron roof, timber walls and a wide veranda running around all four sides. Generous-sized rooms with high ceilings opened on to the verandas and the central hallway, creating cross ventilation, so necessary in summer.

A classic timber archway separated the lounge and dining rooms and all the walls were painted in pale tones, increasing the impression of light and space.

But the decor was very masculine and rather urban, with lots of dark leather and smoky glass and chrome, not quite the cosy country homestead that Nell had anticipated.

'Is it OK if I let Ambrose out of jail?' she asked Jacob.

He grinned. 'Sure.'

She released the catch on the cage and Ambrose approached his freedom cautiously, padding forward on soft paws with his tail high, like a feathery plume, as he explored the lounge room.

'Will the dogs be jealous if he's allowed inside?'

Jacob shook his head and was clearly very confident. 'Not at all. They're well-trained.'

Sharp-eyed Katrina was watching Nell closely. 'What do you think of the house?'

'It's beautiful,' Nell said diplomatically. She smiled warily at Jacob. 'Plenty of room for the three of us.'

'There are four bedrooms and a sleep-out on the veranda,' he said. 'Stacks of room for your quilting stuff.' He returned her smile and she fancied she caught a bright flash of warmth in his eyes, just for her.

Sam squirmed in Jacob's arms and let out a wail.

Nell recognised that cry. 'He needs changing.'

Katrina, smugly important, pointed to a room to their right. 'Hilda set up the cot and changing table in there.'

'Terrific.' Jacob headed in the direction she'd indicated. 'Let's get you comfortable, little mate.'

'Can't Nell take care of him?' Katrina interjected.

Jacob hesitated. Over the past few days he'd become almost as adept at nappy-changing as Nell. Now, he stood in the middle of the hallway, holding Sam while his frowning gaze flashed from one woman to the other.

'You didn't say what brings you out here, Katrina.'

'Oh, I was just passing this way and Hilda mentioned you were coming home today.'

He nodded cautiously. 'Thanks for dropping in.'

Katrina, hands on hips, watched him, watched Nell. Her mouth opened as if she planned to say something else, but then she seemed to change her mind and suddenly retrieved a tiny mobile phone from the pocket of her jeans. After flipping a few numbers and squinting at the phone's screen, she flashed them a triumphant grin. 'Something's come up,' she said. 'Sorry, I can't stay after all.'

Jacob's eyebrows lifted, but he said politely, 'That's a pity. Nell, can you take care of Sam? I'll see you out, Katrina.'

Nell decided that Sam needed a bath after the long and dusty journey. It would make him happy and would keep them both out of Jacob's way while he chatted with Katrina.

She had no trouble locating a bathroom and soon Sam was splashing happily in a few inches of water in the bottom of a big blue bath.

As Nell trickled warm water over his head and tummy, she could hear Katrina's voice coming from the side veranda and the low rumble of Jacob's responses. Fortunately, they were far enough away that she couldn't hear exactly what was being said.

Nell concentrated on Sam, telling him what a good boy he was as he splashed and cooed back at her and at last the voices stopped. Taking a soft, fluffy towel from the bathroom shelf, she scooped Sam up and bundled him in it. He looked impossibly cute and smelled wonderfully clean and soapy and so delicious that she couldn't resist showering him with kisses.

'I have to make the most of my opportunities while you're tiny,' she told him. 'There'll come a day when you won't relish being kissed by your grandma.'

A sound from the doorway startled her. Looking up, she saw Jacob standing there, one hand raised to grip the lintel, another propped on his hip, his expression closely shuttered.

'Oh, hello,' she said. 'I thought a bath would be refreshing for Sam.'

From outside came the sound of a car door closing and an engine revving. As the car moved away from the house, Nell felt a wave of sisterly concern for Katrina.

'I hope you were kind to her, Jacob.'

'I was exceedingly polite.'

Nell knew very well that politeness did not always equate with kindness, but she didn't think it was her place to say so now.

'And no, I haven't slept with her,' Jacob added, answering a question Nell hadn't asked but had certainly pondered. 'I'll start unpacking the car,' he said, turning abruptly, clearly upset or embarrassed. Or both.

Oh, boy. It wasn't the easiest of beginnings.

Nell looked down at Sam, who had found his thumb and had started to suck on it. Whatever the real story about Katrina was, her presence here had brought into sharp focus some home truths that Nell had diligently tried to overlook. No way had Jacob Tucker been celibate for the past twenty years.

And, while she and Jacob might be the same age, Nell knew that men, given half a chance, always went for younger women. Robert's new girlfriend was a perfect example. It was generally accepted that many men, like Jacob, got more interesting as they matured, while women...

Oh, heck, let's face it. Women simply...lose their looks.

Nell was pushing forty. There were stretch marks on her tummy and she was at least a whole dress size bigger than when she'd been nineteen. Perhaps she'd been totally, totally foolish to fantasise about Jacob falling in love with her again.

CHAPTER EIGHT

THE bedrooms at Koomalong were large and cool with French windows opening on to the veranda. Nell was to sleep in a room next to Sam's, while Jacob's room was further down the hallway, closer to the kitchen.

She rather liked her room. It was old-fashioned and feminine with pale rose walls, a deeper rose carpet and soft white floor-length curtains. The double bed was covered in a white spread embroidered with sprigs of flowers and there was an English oak dressing table with a swing mirror and all manner of little drawers.

'This is lovely,' she told Jacob as he piled her suitcases neatly in front of the big silky oak wardrobe.

'Glad you like it. Come and take a look at the sleep-out on the side veranda. See if it will suit as a quilting room.'

It was, she soon discovered, perfect. A long section of veranda on the northern side had been closed in, with deep sash windows that looked out over a long, shady paddock. There was even a big old table there, perfect for laying out fabric and for fiddling with colours and patterns.

'Will this do?' Jacob asked, watching her face carefully.

'It's wonderful. So big. And it has lovely vibes. I'm sure this will be a very inspiring place to work in.' She beamed at him. 'And thank you for showing me this room before you showed me the kitchen.'

He looked surprised. 'I don't expect you to spend much time in the kitchen. I'm happy to do my share of the cooking.'

'Really?' Robert had never cooked so much as an egg.

Jacob was keen to show her more. 'Sam's still asleep, so why don't you come outside and I'll introduce you to the horses. I think you'll love Belladonna, my mare.'

'Oh, yes, your mare is Koomalong's star attraction.'

'She's the main reason you agreed to come here.'

'Exactly.'

Their voices were playful, but when their eyes met the playfulness vanished. A shiver trembled through Nell as she stood, trapped by Jacob's serious gaze.

If he'd looked at her that way when they'd been nineteen, she would have quickly closed the distance between them, thrown her arms around him and kissed him till he smiled at her. They would have ended up laughing in each other's arms, kissing some more, tumbling on to the grass together, making love.

At thirty-nine, Nell was much more careful. Walking towards the door, she said softly, 'Show me the way to these horses.'

At the back of the house there was the usual scattering of farm buildings—a machinery shed built from corrugated iron, garages, a laundry and, beyond these, the stables and a horse paddock.

As they walked, Jacob said, 'In case you were wondering, I'm not expecting any other women to turn up on my doorstep.'

'Oh, I wasn't wondering,' Nell lied. 'I know you can't

have lived like a Trappist monk for the past twenty years.'

His mouth tilted in a crooked smile.

'I must say I'm surprised you've never married,' she continued, probing gently. 'I'm assuming you must have had serious relationships, though. There must have been women you've lived with.'

'Not for more than a few weeks. And there hasn't been anyone since I bought Koomalong.'

Nell stopped walking. 'A few weeks? Is that all? In twenty years?'

He gave an impatient shrug. 'My lifestyle hasn't suited settling down. I've been on the move a lot.'

'So if I stay here for a whole month, I'll be breaking some kind of record?'

'I suppose you will.' Jacob laughed gruffly. 'Of course I'm more settled here.'

She felt compelled to probe further. 'It's sad that you've had trouble committing.'

He shot her a hard look, thrust his hands into his pockets and squared his jaw. 'At least I didn't end up marrying someone simply because it might have been convenient.'

Nell blushed. 'Touché. Point taken.'

She was glad they'd reached the horse paddock and she could turn her attention to the four animals grazing there.

'Oh, they're lovely, Jacob. You've always had a good eye for horses.' She admired their lines and the healthy sheen on their coats. 'Who looked after them while you were away?'

'My neighbour's son was happy to keep an eye on them.'

'And ride them, I'll bet.'

'That was part of the arrangement.'

Nell pointed to the bay mare with a pretty white blaze on her forehead. 'Is this Belladonna?'

'Yes. What do you think of her?'

'Gorgeous lines. Fabulous legs.' Nell held out her hand and Belladonna, curious, came to the fence. Nell laughed as she gently stroked her nose and the horse nuzzled her palm, no doubt hoping for a treat. 'Sorry, Belladonna. I'll bring you something tomorrow.' She smiled into the horse's soft brown eyes. 'She looks sensitive, but rather gentle. I can't wait to ride her.'

'Exactly how long is it since you've ridden?'

It wasn't easy to admit the truth. Nell fiddled with a piece of wire wound around a fence post. 'I'm afraid I haven't ridden a horse since the day I last saw you.'

'That long?' Jacob sounded shocked. 'You'll get very stiff and sore, then.'

'I'll have to take it in gentle stages then, won't I?'

'You will. In very gentle stages.'

Nell looked up, caught the silvery shimmer in Jacob's eyes and her heart did a tumble turn. She was quite sure he was thinking about gentle stages that had nothing to do with riding horses.

Jacob set the wok of stir-fried beef and noodles at the back of the stove and went in search of Nell. She'd been feeding Sam and he wanted to tell her that dinner was ready when she was.

There was a lamp on in the lounge room and an empty feeding bottle on the coffee table, but no sign of Nell or Sam.

He headed down the hall to Sam's room, but was only halfway there when he heard Nell call, 'Jacob, is that you? Come here quickly.'

There was a sharp edge to her voice and he couldn't tell if it was excitement or panic. His heart leapt as he dashed to Sam's doorway. 'What's the matter?'

Sam was lying on the changing table, his bottom half bare, legs kicking. Nell had been laughing at him and she turned to Jacob, her face alight, glowing.

'Sam smiled at me,' she said.

'No kidding?'

'It was a genuine smile. Not an accidental, windy grin, but the real thing. A proper and deliberate smile. Look.'

Jacob stepped closer and Nell leaned over Sam, grinning at him madly. 'Who's a happy little man?' she asked in a high, animated voice.

Almost immediately, Sam's eyes lit up, his arms and legs pumped madly and his face broke into a smile, a broad, no-doubt-about-it, fully-fledged grin that mirrored Nell's.

Jacob let out a deep chuckle of delight. 'How about that? What a great little guy.'

'Doesn't it change him?' Nell said. 'The smile makes him look so grown up, like a real little human being.'

Jacob laughed, leaned forward and pulled an ultra-happy face at Sam and watched him smile back.

'This is his first important milestone—learning to smile, being happy. Doesn't he look gorgeous?' Nell's blue eyes shone with joy and excitement.

She looked luminous.

Jacob swallowed a sudden constriction in his throat. 'Have you any idea how gorgeous *you* look when you're glowing like that?'

Her eyes widened.

Unable to help himself, Jacob lifted a bright strand of her hair that had strayed from its clip and tucked it behind her ear. She stood very still as he traced the curve of her earlobe, caressed the pink warmth of her cheek. She gasped as his thumb brushed the soft underside of her lower lip.

'Nell,' he whispered.

'Jacob?' Her voice sounded faraway, dreamy.

'I told you that I had no romantic agenda for bringing you here.'

'Yes, you did.'

'I lied. I'm sorry.'

A rosy tide spread from her throat to her cheeks. 'You—you—'

'I want to kiss you.'

She smiled shakily. 'But—'

'No buts.' He touched a finger to her lips. 'I have never wanted anything more.' He'd wanted to kiss her for days, had been going crazy with wanting her. 'It's going to happen, Nell.'

She offered no resistance as he drew her in to him and, with gentle, devastating purpose, touched his lips to hers…

Ah, yes…she was so soft and sweet and tantalising.

Nothing mattered but this.

Nell.

He gathered her closer and kissed her less gently, teased her lips apart with his tongue and Nell was warm and pliant and melting into him. Her arms wound around his neck, her breasts pressed against him and her lips parted freely, welcoming him, urging him to deepen the kiss.

At last…

At long, long last…

Nell in his arms—his fiery, passionate Nell. A storm broke inside Jacob. He closed his eyes, let his senses drown in her.

This was how Nell tasted and how she kissed. These eager lips were her lips, this wonderful, womanly body hers.

How had he survived all these years without tasting and touching and loving Nell?

His fever was contagious. Nell threaded frantic fingers through his hair and wriggled closer, drawing him deeper and deeper into their private maelstrom. He cupped the fullness of her breasts through the soft cotton of her T-shirt, grazed his thumbs over their tips, and she moaned softly, destroying the last shreds of his control.

Beside them on the changing table, Sam let out a squawk of protest.

Nell stiffened as if she'd been shot. She pulled back. 'Oh, goodness.'

She pressed a hand to her throat, was panting a little as she looked down at Sam, who was bellowing now.

'Hush, Sam, what's the matter?' She lifted him up and soothed him. 'There, there. Were you getting cold? You're all right.' Over her shoulder she shot Jacob a gentle reproach. 'He might have fallen off the table.'

Too happy about their kiss, Jacob merely smiled. 'He was quite safe. He can't roll over yet.' With a hand at her waist, he said, 'Why don't we put him down and try that again?'

It was not the best joke he'd ever cracked and he realised that the spell, if that was what it had been, was already broken. Nell grabbed the chance to resume her former composure.

'Just behave,' she said, pushing him gently in the chest with both hands. 'And remember—'

'What? Remember what?'

She surprised him by kissing him quickly. 'We're all on probation here.'

Oh, yeah…

He supposed he'd spoil everything by rushing in fool-ishly, the way he had when they were young.

Sam had stopped crying and Nell laid him back on the changing table. Deftly she closed the tapes on his nappy and snapped the little studs on his sleeping suit.

'You're a dab hand at that now,' Jacob said. 'By the way, dinner's ready whenever you are.'

'Lovely. Thanks.' She gave him a grateful smile.

He knew he wasn't mistaken. There was an extra-happy light in her eyes that hadn't been there before.

'You're a good cook,' Nell said as they ate their evening meal at the scrubbed pine table in the kitchen. 'I suppose your mother taught you.'

'Yes, she seemed to enjoy passing on what she knew.'

'Maggie's a gifted teacher. Much better than the ones I had when I went to adult education classes.'

Jacob's eyebrows lifted. 'I've been meaning to ask. Why didn't you finish your university degree?'

She shook her head. 'I'm afraid I lost my enthusiasm for the arts.'

'But you loved your studies. You were mad about poetry.'

'I know, but... I took a job in a city bookshop.'

'OK.' He pulled a face as he accepted this. 'Is that when you started the adult education classes?'

'No, that came later. After I was married. I began with cooking classes because Robert wanted me to give dinner parties. And then I took classes in garden design and interior decorating so that our place in Toorak could look just right.' She rolled her eyes. 'It had to be *the very latest thing, darling*.'

'That doesn't sound like you.'

'I know. And then there was public speaking.'

Jacob looked shocked. 'Public speaking?'

She laughed nervously. 'I wasn't actually planning to speak in public, but I wanted to be more confident when I was talking to Robert's barrister friends.'

'For crying out loud. You were full of confidence when I knew you.'

'Was I?' She shrugged and said uneasily, 'That was different. Moving in Robert's circle, I felt I needed classes to help me to express opinions without sounding apologetic.'

This was greeted by silence.

Embarrassed that she'd revealed too much, Nell traced the willow pattern on her plate with her fork.

He said softly, 'I'm glad none of that really changed you, Nell.'

She looked up to find him smiling at her.

'Maybe you think that because I'm back in the bush.' She sent him a cheeky grin. 'I'm reverting to type.'

'Whatever the reason, I'm exceedingly grateful.'

It was one of those shining moments of connection, of *knowing*. Nell was on the brink of leaving her chair. Every instinct urged her to walk to the other end of the table, put her arms around Jacob and kiss him. But from beyond the kitchen came a wail from Sam.

And then there were more wails in quick succession.

She smiled ruefully. 'Sounds like he's going to have one of his restless nights.'

They spent the rest of the evening taking it in turns to pace with Sam while finishing their meal and tidying the kitchen. By the time they finally got Sam back to sleep, Nell was exhausted.

'You look dead on your feet,' Jacob told her. 'It's been a long journey today. Get to bed.'

* * *

The next day was set aside for settling in properly, finishing unpacking and taking a quick tour of the property and in the cool of the afternoon Jacob volunteered to mind Sam while Nell took Belladonna for a short ride.

'Are you sure you'll be OK with Sam?' she asked for the hundredth time.

'Of course. Anyway, you won't be gone long.'

'If he fusses, put him on the floor in the lounge room for a kick. I did that this morning and he loves it.'

'I'll remember. Now *you* remember to take it easy.' Jacob checked her saddle and girth straps and bridle as many times as Nell had quizzed him about Sam. 'It's a long, long time since you've ridden.'

She took Belladonna for a lap around the paddock to prove she still knew how to stay on a horse and Jacob was satisfied.

'I'll just take her down to the creek,' Nell said. 'I might sit there for a bit and enjoy the peace of the bush.'

'Why not? I guess it's a long time since you last sat on a creek bank.'

Nell nudged Belladonna forward.

'Keep out of tree branches,' Jacob called.

She smiled and waved and Belladonna broke into a canter and then a gallop.

Now *this* was living—the sense of gathering speed and the powerful rhythm of a beautiful animal beneath her. There was nothing Nell loved more than the rush of wind in her face, the smell of dust stirred by the horse's hooves, the hint of eucalyptus.

She reached the creek quite quickly. Too quickly. She would have loved to continue, but she knew she would pay sorely if she went too far. Reining Belladonna to a walk, she continued along the high bank until she reached a point where the creek widened into a quiet pool.

With the reins securely tied to a tree branch, she sat on a smooth, sun-warmed rock and stared down at the water. It was so still she could see the sky reflected in it. There was a tangle of gnarled tree roots sticking up in the middle of the pool, no doubt washed downstream by the heavy rains of a previous summer. On the far side a lone white heron fished the shallows.

There was nothing special about the scene. It could have been any ordinary old creek anywhere in the Outback. But sitting there, alone, on a shelf of pink granite rock, looking out at the tea-coloured water, at the endless stretch of dry red earth and the wide, clean skies, Nell heard the call of a warbling magpie and felt hot tears stinging her eyes.

She swiped at them with the backs of her hands and was able to laugh. What a nostalgic old granny she'd become.

It was close to dark by the time she got back. The light was fading and in the horse yard behind the stables she couldn't see properly to undo Belladonna's saddle. She had to feel for the buckles and the girth strap and she lifted the saddle high to avoid hitting the horse's back. Then she hung the saddle and blanket on a fence railing, before carefully testing Belladonna's hooves with her fingers to check for stones.

Satisfied that all was well, she turned the mare loose in the paddock and stowed the saddle in the tack room.

From the house, the warm glow of the kitchen lights spooled out into the twilight-shrouded backyard and, as she crossed the lawn, she hoped Sam had been on his best behaviour for Jacob.

Suddenly a cat's screech and a cacophony of barking disrupted the peaceful twilight. Ahead of her, a marmalade streak shot up the back steps, with Jacob's dogs tearing after it. The kitchen door must have been unlatched, for it swung forward and all three animals burst inside, the dogs barking so loudly they sounded demented.

What an uproar! The dogs weren't allowed inside the house and, in this frenzy, they could wreck the place. Nell hurried after them.

As she reached the back steps, she heard Sam's piercing cries in addition to the frenzied barking and the ear-splitting yowls of feline terror.

She dashed through the kitchen, dimly aware of appetising cooking smells and that the table had been set with a bright seersucker cloth. She followed the noise through to the lounge room, taking in the scene at a glance.

Jacob was standing in the middle of the room, holding a red-faced, screaming Sam and Ambrose was halfway up the wall, clinging to the curtain. The cat's teeth were bared and his tail bristled fiercely as he gripped the silky fabric for dear life while the dogs leapt and barked up at him.

Then Jacob lent his voice to the general mêlée.

'Blue! Dander!' he roared at the dogs. 'Get out of here. Now!'

Unfortunately, the normally obedient animals were whipped into too great a passion and took absolutely no notice of their master.

Nell stepped into the fray, arms outstretched. 'Give me Sam,' she called.

Jacob spun around. His eyes widened when he saw her, but she couldn't tell if he was relieved or dismayed that she'd caught him in the middle of this dilemma.

She hurried forward. 'Here, I'll take Sam.'

He thrust the wailing baby at her. 'Thanks.' Then he

dashed across the room and grabbed the Labrador by the collar. 'Sit!' he ordered.

The dog immediately stopped barking. He gave Jacob one brief look of outrage at being deprived of such fantastic fun, then sat.

'You, too,' Jacob ordered the blue cattle dog. 'Sit!'

And suddenly the only sounds in the room were Sam's terrified screams.

'There, there,' Nell soothed him and cuddled him close. 'You're OK now, sweetheart. Shh.'

'Out!' Jacob addressed the dogs and pointed to the doorway and, to everyone's relief, they obediently trotted forward. But they kept looking back, like children sent to their rooms for misbehaving, hoping Jacob's hard heart would soften and set them free to torment Ambrose again.

When the dogs were safely outside at last, Jacob turned to Nell. Sam was still snuffling and sobbing against her neck, but she had managed to reduce his terror.

'What happened?' she asked, patting his little back.

Jacob's eyebrows rose as he scratched his head. 'Blowed if I know. The dogs have been so good about the cat.' He looked up at Ambrose, still clinging to the curtain. 'Better get you down, mate.' Reaching high, he clasped Ambrose around the middle with one hand while he prised his claws from the fabric.

And then Jacob stood facing Nell, looking embarrassed and cradling the cat in his arms in much the same way that she was holding Sam.

'Is Ambrose OK?'

'Seems fine.' Jacob checked one fluffy orange flank and then the other. 'No sign of blood or missing fur.'

'That's good. Poor fellow. I think the fight started near

the back steps. Maybe Ambrose tried to eat out of one of the dog's bowls.'

'You could be right.' Jacob gave the cat a thoughtful scratch between the ears. 'My fault. I forgot to feed him.'

Nell gave him a small smile. 'You've been busy dealing with Sam and dinner.'

'Yeah.' Ambrose twisted in his hands and Jacob was forced to release him on to the floor. As the cat began to wash himself, Jacob straightened and looked at Nell. 'Did you have a good ride?'

'It was wonderful, thanks.'

'Not too stiff?'

'Not so far.'

He had never looked more gorgeous as he stood there in battered old jeans and an equally old T-shirt with a hole near the neck. If she hadn't been holding Sam she might have dashed across the room and hurled herself into his arms, told him how very much she'd wished he'd been with her down at the creek.

But Sam began to fret. 'Did he behave for you?' she remembered to ask.

'He was just starting to grizzle before the cat and the dogs arrived.'

'I guess he's due for his evening bottle.'

'I'll take care of that.'

'But you've already done your share.'

'You need to soak in a warm bath. If you don't relax your muscles after the ride, you'll be sorry.' Jacob was wearing his masterful look now. 'After, with luck, we might be able to enjoy a drink before dinner.'

With meek thanks, Nell headed for the bathroom and, half an hour later, feeling wonderfully warm and clean and relaxed, she found the lounge room restored and Jacob pouring two glasses of chilled wine.

'Is Sam asleep?'

'Out like a light.' He handed her a glass. 'Take the weight off your feet.'

She sank gratefully into an armchair. 'This is very civilised.' She sipped her wine and wondered why she wasn't calm. She'd just had a beautifully relaxing bath and surely, by now, she should be able to sit in a room with Jacob Tucker without feeling as if she might swoon at any moment.

Jacob, on the other hand, seemed excessively calm, with his mind on other things entirely. 'Be honest,' he said with a sweeping gesture that took in their surroundings. 'Tell me what you think of this room.'

Nell followed his gaze. 'It's lovely and big.'

'What about the furniture?'

'It's very—' She hesitated.

'It feels like office furniture?' he finished for her.

'Perhaps,' she said carefully.

'It doesn't really feel like a home?' he prompted.

Nell nodded thoughtfully.

He angled a wry grin. 'If you'd decorated it, would you have used all this leather and chrome?'

'I tend to go for a more traditional look,' she admitted. 'This is such a lovely old timber home. I'd probably fill it with comfy chintz lounges and deckle-edged mirrors, lots more timber and antique furniture.' She smiled at him. 'I have something that might help to warm this room up a little.'

'Yeah?' He was intrigued.

'I'll be back in a minute.'

She hurried into her new sewing room and came back with her arms full of quilts.

'You could think about hanging one of these on the wall,' she said. 'Or even, if you draped one over the sofa, it would help to soften the starkness of the dark leather.'

With a flick of her arm, she opened a quilt and tossed it over the sofa. It was one of her favourites, a carefully pieced, dramatic blend of ochre, cream, aqua and green.

'Wow! That's beautiful!' Setting his glass aside, Jacob stood and examined the quilt more closely. He picked up a corner and fingered a fine seam. 'You're so talented, Nell. And it's the perfect colour combination for here. The colours of the Outback.'

'I made it once when I was feeling homesick for the bush.' She held it up against a blank wall. 'It goes well with this room, doesn't it? You could hang it here, or above the sideboard.'

'It would look stunning.'

'I have some leftover fabric. I could make throw cushions to match.'

'I wouldn't want to put you to too much trouble.'

'It's no trouble. Quilting's my thing. Honestly, I love it. I find it very comforting to be able to plan a whole quilt and have it turn out exactly the way I wanted it to.' She laughed. 'See? I'm a control freak.'

'You're a genius.'

Before she realised quite what was happening, Jacob was swinging her off her feet and the quilt dropped from her hands.

A laugh bubbled from her. 'I'm glad you like my quilts.'

'I like a damn sight more than your quilts, my girl.'

Their faces were inches apart. Nell was instantly ablaze as she looked into Jacob's eyes and saw his unguarded desire.

'I'm very taken with everything about you, Nell,' he said softly as he lowered her to the floor. 'Your quilts, your smile, the way you look when you hold Sam, the way you look right now.'

'How do I look right now?'

He squinted and pretended to study her. 'I'd say you look…like an incredibly sexy grandmother.'

She laughed again. 'Don't I look like a happy grandmother?'

His eyes shimmered. 'That, too.'

'I'm remarkably happy, Jacob.'

He framed her face with his hands. 'Any idea about the cause of all this happiness?'

'Oh, I think I like being here.'

'Here?' He dropped a tiny kiss on her brow.

'Right here,' she breathed, lifting her lips to kiss the roughness of his jaw.

'Anything special about here?' Jacob asked as he pressed his lips to her eyelids.

Nell was burning up. Any minute now, she would be a pile of cinders on the floor.

'Tell me,' he insisted as his lips roamed close to her ear.

She whispered, 'I'm rather partial to the way you kiss.'

'Great answer, Nell.'

Jacob's arms wrapped around her and he covered her open lips with his.

As soon as their mouths met, they both knew that tonight kisses would not be enough. Greedily, their hands sought to touch and explore and their bodies strained together, pressing in with an urgent and greedy precision.

'Come with me,' Jacob murmured, kissing her mouth, her jaw, her throat.

Anywhere, anywhere…she answered silently. And in a haze of heat she went with him down the hallway, through a doorway and into his bedroom.

CHAPTER NINE

IT WAS only then, when Nell saw Jacob's lamp-lit room, his enormous bed with its solid timber headboard, its scattering of silver and grey pillows and huge black duvet, that she felt a splash of cold dismay. This was the first time she'd been with a man since her divorce.

Jacob sensed her hesitation. 'What's the matter, Nell?'

'I'm—' she swallowed the nervous blockage in her throat '—I'm so old now.'

He threw back his head and laughed. 'You're no older than I am.'

'It's different for a woman. Age matters more, makes more of a change.'

'Rubbish,' he muttered thickly and he pulled her towards him. 'Come here and tell me you're old.'

Against his shoulder, she protested, 'I'm certainly not the nubile girl you seduced.'

'Of course you're not. You're even lovelier, Nell.'

'I'm nearly forty.'

'So what?' Jacob kissed her jaw, her earlobe, buried his face in her neck. 'You smell nineteen.'

She couldn't help laughing. Jacob had always made her laugh. 'That's because I used Sam's baby soap.'

'I'll buy a truckload of Sam's baby soap.' He kissed her mouth, nibbled at her lower lip and stilled her laughter, sending fresh flames of longing coursing through her. 'You taste like my Nell.'

Oh, Jacob, you darling man.

His hands gripped her bottom and he held her against his hardness. 'You feel like my Nell.'

A soft groan came from him, a small whimper from her. He dipped his mouth lower.

Nell was grateful for the subdued lamplight as his hands slipped under her T shirt, guided it up and over her head.

Oh, gosh. Why hadn't she thought to wear a sexy bra, something lacy and pretty, instead of this plain white cotton? But apparently it didn't matter. Jacob was too busy hauling his T-shirt off. How magnificent his chest was. Such shoulders.

Then he was kissing her again, steering her backwards till her trembling legs met his bed. He eased her down to the mattress, joined her there, helped her out of her bra. And he was so enraptured by what he found that Nell forgot to worry about how round and pale her body was, forgot to worry about anything.

Her eyes drifted closed, her mouth fell open in a soundless exclamation as Jacob paid flattering homage to her femininity. She was nineteen again, head over heels in love with this man, wanting only this man.

And *how* she wanted him.

In a fever of haste they shed the rest of their clothing. A happy little cry escaped her as they came together once more, rolling into each other's embrace, desperate to savour the electrifying thrill of skin against skin, of Jacob's rigid nakedness against her soft contours.

He hugged her to him. 'You're beautiful, Nell. You're gorgeous. You haven't changed a bit.' Easing back a little, he traced the curve of her hip. 'All woman,' he murmured. And then, 'Ah, there it is.'

'What is?'

'The little butterfly-shaped birthmark on your hip.'

Bending forward, he kissed the spot on her hip, making a warm circle with his lips and his tongue. Longing and happy memories swept over Nell as he trailed kisses from the dip of her waist to the swell of her breast.

She fleetingly marvelled that everything was happening so easily. There was nothing awkward or jarring to hinder them and they found ways to please each other with surprising ease. Every touch, every kiss was fuel to the fire of their longing.

When Jacob paused to reach into a drawer in his bedside table, Nell almost protested. She felt so gloriously reckless she wanted to throw caution to the wind. But then sanity returned. After all, she was almost forty. They had a grandson.

And all she wanted now was Jacob.

She watched his eyes as he joined her, saw deep emotion married to dark hunger. Then she closed her eyes and cried his name once before she was submerged in a spiralling whirlpool of need.

She lay with her head on his shoulder. 'That was amazing.'

Jacob dropped a kiss on her forehead. 'I felt so close to you.'

Nell pressed her lips into his neck, tasted the salt on his skin. 'I didn't expect to be so uninhibited.'

He smiled at her. 'That's because this is where we're meant

to be.' He let his hand trail down her arm, then drew a circle over her stomach. 'And this is where our little baby grew.'

'Yes.' The monosyllable caught in her throat.

He pressed his splayed hand gently against her stomach and she watched the darkness of his skin against the paleness of hers. She felt the warmth of him there, awakening memories of her pregnancy, of the weight of the baby inside her, the strong little limbs kicking.

The awful loss…

'Oh, Jacob.'

She wanted to tell him about Tegan, about her pregnancy and how she'd felt while carrying their child, but, without warning, tears spilled.

'What is it, Nell? What's the matter?'

'I loved Tegan.'

'I know, sweetheart. I know.'

'Even before she was born, I loved her so much.'

Suddenly, she was weeping—weeping for the loss of her baby and for the loss of this man whom she'd loved more than anything in the world. In one fell sweep she'd lost everyone who had mattered. And now Tegan was gone forever.

Jacob held her tightly and buried his face in her hair. She wasn't sure if he was weeping too, but they clung to each other, rocking gently, sharing the pain they'd borne for too long, offering the comfort that only they could give.

It was quite a long while before the flow of Nell's tears stopped, but she felt awed by a sweet sense of release, as if the crying had cleansed her.

She looked at Jacob in the faint lamplight, gave him a shaky smile.

He smiled back at her, kissed her nose, her damp cheeks and eyelids. 'Everything's going to be OK now, Nell.'

'Yes, I know.'

This was a new beginning.

'Roll over,' he said. 'I'll give you a massage.'

'There's no need. I'm OK now.'

'Roll over.'

Shooting him a shy smile, Nell obeyed. And very soon she was inexpressibly grateful as his warm hands rubbed and kneaded her back, soothing and freeing muscles that she hadn't realised had become tense, dropping warm kisses wherever he rubbed. She could feel her body relaxing and letting go, felt happiness spreading through her again like warmed honey.

Until gradually the tempo and rhythm of the massage changed. Jacob's hands slowed and his fingers began to trace gentle, dreamy circles on her back. He trailed feather-soft caresses down her spine to her buttocks and thighs and a new thrilling tension blossomed in Nell.

Rolling on to her side, she whispered, 'My turn.'

'You want to give me a massage?'

'More or less,' she replied, running seeking fingers over his magnificent chest, venturing lower. 'On your back, man.'

Jacob did as he was told.

He felt *so-o-o* good. Nell gloried in him, reawakening suppressed memories as her hands explored eagerly, redis-covering the wonder of his satiny skin stretched smooth and taut over masculine muscles, adding bold kisses wherever she touched him.

Soon it grew too much for Jacob and he took control again, moving over her, lavishing her with kisses as he took her, once more, to the moon.

When Sam woke it was still dark. His wails penetrated Nell's sleep and she sat up quickly, her heart racing. She didn't think she'd been asleep for very long, but it had been long enough for her to feel confused by her surroundings. She took a moment or two to remember she was in Jacob's room. In his bed.

He stirred beside her. 'Is that Sam?' he asked sleepily.

'Yes. He'll be hungry.' Nell yawned and her stomach rumbled. 'Actually, I'm hungry too.'

'That's because we forgot to eat dinner.'

'Oh, heavens, you were cooking something. What happened to it?'

'I turned the heat off while you were in the bath. I'm afraid the casserole's still in the oven.'

She giggled. 'It might still be OK. I'll check while I'm warming Sam's bottle. If it's burned, I might fix a snack. Do you fancy cheese on toast?'

'Sure. I'll help you make it.'

Nell was so used to the 'wifely' role she'd played during her marriage that she almost ordered Jacob to stay where he was, but he was already rolling out of his side of the bed. She wondered where her T-shirt was, switched on the lamp and saw it lying on the floor near the door. Actually, there were articles of clothing scattered all over the floor.

'Look at this room,' she cried, smacking her hand to her forehead in mock dismay. 'What shocking behaviour. You'd think grandparents would set a better example.'

'Some old folk have no sense of decorum,' Jacob agreed solemnly.

It became a pattern.

In the nights that followed, if Sam woke around two a.m., Jacob would grumble, but then good-naturedly head for the kitchen to heat his bottle while Nell changed the baby and brought him back to their bed. They would talk softly, weave dreams for Sam while he drank, brought up wind and fell back to sleep again, making soft baby sounds as he snuggled between them.

During the day, Jacob had work to attend to around the property but, as he still had cattle scattered on agistments around the state, his holding at Koomalong was relatively small and manageable and he made time to be with his new little family.

One day they had a picnic. Jacob and Nell took Sam in his basket and cooked sausages over a fire beside the creek. On another day they went for a long walk through the bush with Sam in a baby sling and the dogs hard at their heels. They even went riding together and Jacob carried Sam in the sling.

Many evenings, they spent on the western veranda, Ambrose purring, Sam in Nell's lap, or being walked up and down if he was restless. Jacob's dogs sprawled at their feet while they watched the sun drip molten gold as it sank into the distant hills and they listened to corellas and cockatiels calling to each other as they winged their way homewards through the purple light.

In the evenings, they cooked together in the homestead kitchen, experimenting with new pasta dishes, a fancy stir-fry or risotto.

Nell wrote a long letter to Jean to keep her abreast of Sam's latest antics. He was piling on weight and he smiled all the time now. He could hold his rattle and he was very close to rolling over from his back to his tummy. She spoke to Jacob's mother, who rang one night from the Kimberley and they had a long and cosy chat, just like the old times when they'd talked in the kitchen at Half Moon.

When Hilda Knowles, Jacob's cleaning woman, came to do the ironing and to give the house its weekly 'once-over', she made it quite clear that she very much approved of Nell.

'I've never seen Mr Tucker looking so well,' she confided.

Nell looked up from folding Sam's freshly laundered clothes. 'Has Jacob been ill?'

'Not ill, no. He's always been as fit as a fiddle. Perhaps *well* isn't quite the right word.'

Hilda set the iron to rest and her brow puckered while she gave Jacob's condition careful thought. 'There's always been something in his eyes that troubled me. A sadness. A kind of shadow. And it's gone now. When he smiles, his eyes light up as if there's a constant happy glow inside him. I reckon you must have put that there, love.'

Nell fervently hoped so, but neither she nor Jacob talked aloud about their Koomalong experiment. No doubt they were both frightened that talking about it might break the magic spell. But secretly she was confident that things were working out just fine.

The parcel from Jean arrived in the third week.

Sam was awake after his morning nap and he was kicking on a blanket on the lounge room floor when the mail truck's horn sounded. Most of the envelopes were addressed to Jacob, but there was a large rectangular parcel for Nell and she brought it into the lounge room to sit on the floor beside Sam as she unwrapped layers of brown paper.

Inside was a box covered with a collage of pictures cut from magazines—the kind of collage a child might create with pictures of rock stars, sporting heroes and film stars mixed in with whales, dolphins and baby seals.

Mystified, Nell opened the box and found a pile of Christmas and birthday cards—all the cards she had ever sent to Tegan.

Jean had written:

I was cleaning out Tegan's room when I found these and I thought you should have them. There is one we need to talk about.

'She kept them all,' Nell whispered, her throat tightening as the truth of this sank in.

Tegan had kept every single card that Nell had ever sent, all of them, right back to the card covered in mischievous tabby kittens, sent for her daughter's fifth birthday.

Nell had completely forgotten that card, but now, seeing those cheeky kittens playing with a ball of red wool, she could remember exactly how she'd felt when she'd bought it. She could recall the ages she'd spent in the newsagent's before making that selection, the agonies she'd gone through trying to decide what to write inside.

Finally, she'd settled on a very simple message: *Happy Birthday, dear Tegan. Love, Nell.* She'd only ever signed her name as Nell.

Now, as she sifted through the cards she'd sent, she

felt renewed gratitude to Jean who'd allowed this precious contact.

How carefully she'd selected these cards. When Tegan had been small there'd been cute cards with fairies and flowers, kittens, puppies and ducklings. As her daughter had grown older Nell had chosen funny cards, or ones she'd hoped were funny, then something 'cool' during the teenage years.

At Christmas Nell had always sent Tegan an 'Australiana' card—beautiful scenes from the Outback, a gentle nudge to acquaint her daughter with her natural roots—creamy paperbarks beside a quiet billabong, a dog on a tucker box, gum-trees, blue hills at the edge of a flat, red plain.

Nell frowned as she reached the last Christmas card she'd sent Tegan. There was something tucked inside it—folded sheets of writing paper.

Puzzled, she unfolded the pages, then realised they were nothing to do with her. This was a letter for Tegan, written closely in a spiky, masculine hand. Goosebumps broke out on Nell's skin as she recognised Jacob's handwriting.

She shouldn't read this. But it was already too late. Her eyes had skimmed the opening paragraph, the first page.

Dear Tegan,

I can never thank you enough for writing to me. You have no idea what it meant to hear from you and I'm so happy to know you're alive and well. I have a daughter!!!! How fabulous is that?

At last I know what became of my child.

I understand that you must wonder why you were given up for adoption. Believe me, Tegan, I did not

*want to lose you. I wanted you. You are the result of
my love for a very special woman. I planned to
provide for you, to care for you and your mother, but
circumstances beyond my control intervened.*

Nell's vision blurred.

She couldn't bear this. Jacob's letter was so sweet, but
she shouldn't go on to read the next page. Tears fell as she
folded it and slipped it back inside the envelope.

Had Jean Browne known Jacob's letter was there? Had
she read it?

Wiping her eyes with the backs of her hands, Nell
looked down at Sam, kicking on the rug, batting his hands
in the air as he tried to reach the bright, stuffed Humpty
Dumpty that Jacob had bought him. The baby saw her
looking at him and his little face broke into a grin.

Oh, the sweetheart.

The dear little man. Nell scooped him up and cuddled him
close. How warm and alive and delightfully chubby he was.

Tegan's bonny little boy.

With the baby in her lap, she tidied the cards and picked
up the box to return them but, as she lifted the lid, she saw
something that she'd missed earlier.

A white envelope with a note attached by a paper-clip.

*I only found this today, when I finally cleaned out
Tegan's desk. I thought it would be best if you and
Jacob read it first and then we need to talk, to work
out what to do.*

The envelope was addressed in round, girlish handwriting in purple ink and it was addressed to Mr Mitch Bradley

who lived, apparently, in a suburb of Sydney. Tegan's address was on the back and the letter was stamped, but there was no postmark.

Mitch Bradley.

Nell had never heard of him, but she felt a ghostly premonition as she stared at the envelope. Why did Jean think this letter was so important?

Could he be Sam's father?

She was suddenly afraid. Sam's father.

Sam's father could threaten their happy little family.

Not again. Please, no, not Sam. I can't lose him, too.

The seal on the envelope had been broken and Nell could feel the sheets of stationery inside, but she couldn't bring herself to open it.

As she sat there, her hands shaking with her indecision, she was saved by the growl of an engine outside. Jacob had been checking fences and feeding supplements to his heifers in the breeder paddock and now he was back. Quickly, Nell stuffed the cards and letters into the box and closed the lid firmly.

With Sam in her arms, she straightened her shoulders, determined to be cheerful. She'd prepared a salad for their lunch, cold chicken and avocado. She would let Jacob enjoy his meal before she told him about the unsettling puzzle that had arrived in the mail.

Her heart gave a tiny, love-sick lurch as she watched him swing out of his truck and take the back stairs two at a time.

'And how are my two favourite people?' he asked, dropping a kiss on Nell's cheek and another on the top of Sam's head.

'We're as happy as fleas.' Nell dredged up a show of gaiety. But perhaps she wasn't very convincing. Jacob's eyes narrowed. 'Fleas?' He smiled carefully, and asked cautiously, 'And how happy are they?'

Nell offered a smile in reply and gave a little shrug. 'How were your heifers and fences?' she asked, hoping to deflect him.

'The heifers are fine. But a few sections of fence needed mending.' He frowned, looked directly into her eyes. 'Are you sure you're OK? You seem tense somehow.'

'I'm fine. Go and get cleaned up. Lunch is almost ready.'

Nell put Sam in the baby swing they'd set up at one end of the kitchen and she set the table and took the salad from the fridge, added dressing and tossed it. Wished she felt calmer.

Having grown up at Half Moon, she knew the right questions to ask Jacob about the property, so while they ate she quizzed him about the bores and the pasture and the condition of the heifers. Unfortunately, Jacob wasn't easily deceived.

When the meal was almost finished and they were drinking tea, he challenged her again. 'There's something bothering you, Nell.'

Perhaps it was best to get this over with. 'Something came in the mail from Jean. Bring your tea into the lounge room. It's all in there.'

Her stomach tied itself in knots as Jacob followed her. 'Jean Browne sent me this box,' she explained, taking the lid off and showing Jacob the contents. 'These are all the cards I sent Tegan, and there's a letter.' Quickly she located the card in the pile with Jacob's letter inside it.

She handed it to him and watched his face as he unfolded the notepaper and recognised his writing. She saw his strong features tighten and the muscles in his throat work. When he looked up, his eyes were extra bright.

'You read this?' he asked quietly.

'Only the beginning. I'm sorry. I'd started reading before I realised what it was.'

He shook his head. 'I don't mind. It's only the truth about how I felt.' Carefully, he refolded the letter and slipped it into his shirt pocket, then looked at her with a worried frown. 'Is that what you're upset about?'

'No, not that. I thought what you wrote was beautiful.' Nell showed him the envelope. 'There was another letter.'

She held her breath as Jacob read Jean's note and then the address, turned the envelope over and read Tegan's sender details.

'You haven't read this one?'

'No. I was getting up the nerve when you arrived back.'

He tapped a brown finger against the front of the envelope. 'You know who this Mitch Bradley probably is, don't you?'

She swallowed a prickle of fear. 'I suppose he might be Sam's father.'

'I'd say there's a fair chance.'

For a long moment they stared at each other and Nell knew Jacob's thoughts echoed hers. These thin sheets of paper could reveal the one person in the world who could take Sam away from them.

'We'd better have a look at it,' Jacob said with the carefully composed expression of a doctor discussing his patient's need for open heart surgery.

'I wish we didn't have to.' Nell's voice vibrated querulously.

'We don't have any choice, Nell.'

She knew Jacob was right, but she felt ill. How could she bear to lose Sam?

From the kitchen came the sound of his whimpers.

She said, 'You read the letter while I get the baby.' It was cowardly to be scared, but she couldn't help it. She was glad to escape.

Sam needed changing and she took her time attending to him, gave him an extra cuddle and fetched a bottle of boiled water for him to drink.

When she returned to the lounge room, Jacob was sitting in a deep leather armchair, his expression sombre. 'You'd better read it,' he said.

A disturbing light in his eyes made her heart leap. 'Is Mitch Bradley the father?'

Jacob nodded.

Nell groaned as she pictured an angry young man storming Koomalong, sweeping Sam out of her arms and out of their lives.

'I'll take Sam while you read it,' Jacob said, holding the letter out to her.

It was not a fair exchange, Nell thought. Her arms felt empty as she gave Sam up and she fumbled trying to prise the pages out of the envelope. Her heart hammered as she sank on to the sofa and began to read.

Dear Mitch,
This letter has been a long time coming, so long that you might have forgotten what happened when we picked peaches together in Beechworth last summer. I went to that raging Christmas party with you. Remember?

I've written so many letters and torn them up. I

hope this time I'll get the words down without panicking. The thing is, I've had a baby, Mitch. He's almost six weeks old, so if you do your maths you'll see that I fell pregnant at the end of November.

OK, I'm sweating telling you this, but you're the father. I know this will be a shock because we took precautions, but something must have gone wrong. I swear I didn't sleep with anyone else the whole summer.

I very nearly didn't tell you, because I understand this will not be good news for you. I know you were only picking fruit for a few weeks and then heading back to Sydney to join your rock band and the whole father bit will totally wreck your life.

But I'm adopted, you see. I don't think I mentioned that before. And just recently I had a letter from my father—my real father. It blew me away. He's so cool. All this time I never knew him and he sounds like the greatest guy. A cattleman. I can't wait to meet him.

Then I started thinking about Sam, my little baby, and how he will never know his father and how sad that's going to be for him.

Don't panic. I don't expect you to marry me or anything insane like that. But you do have a right to know about your son.

After that, it's up to you.

I might be too busy to write again because Sam keeps me really busy, but at least now you have my address.

Hope you're not too bummed by this.

Luv,

Tegan.

Nell looked up from the letter.

Jacob's face was solemn as he watched her. 'It's dated the day before the accident.'

'Is it?' She hadn't taken any notice of the date and now she turned back to the first page and saw that he was right. 'Poor Tegan.'

'Poor Mitch.'

'He's in for a shock.'

But she was shocked, too. Her gaze flew to Sam, who looked so adorably cute and comfortable in Jacob's strong arms. So at home, so right.

She tossed the letter on to the coffee table. 'It's so unfair to learn about this now.' She snatched up a cushion and hugged it to her chest. 'I've fallen completely in love with Sam.'

'I know. I know…' Jacob sighed heavily. 'But we'll have to talk to this Mitch Bradley. He's obviously Sam's father.'

'What if he wants to contest Sam's custody? I couldn't stand it.' Nell knew she sounded petulant, but she couldn't help it. 'It sounds as if he's in a rock band. He's probably as irresponsible as they come.'

'We don't know that, do we? You're prejudging the bloke.'

Was she? Was she really? How could Tegan's foot-loose young boyfriend have the same longing to care for Sam that she had?

'Jacob, don't you care that this Mitch guy might try to take Sam away from us?'

'Of course I do.'

He looked sad and too impossibly gorgeous, sitting there with Sam in his arms. Nell closed her eyes and struggled to think clearly, without bias. But she couldn't get past the mind-numbing thought that she and Jacob were facing the possibility of losing Sam, that the fragile dynamics of their relationship were completely threatened.

They'd only had a few short weeks, had just started to get to know each other after twenty years.

And the reality was that Jacob had only invited her to Koomalong because of Sam. She and Jacob were only back together because of Sam.

If Sam was taken out of the equation...

She couldn't bear to think about it.

Sam squirmed in Jacob's arms and she jumped at the chance to escape before she blurted out her fears and Jacob confirmed them. 'I'd better take him now. It's time for his feed, and then his naptime.'

Jacob felt as if he'd been slammed by a ten ton truck as he watched Nell leave the room.

In theory, he'd applauded the idea of finding Sam's father. He'd spent twenty years in the dark before discovering he had a daughter and he didn't want to see another guy suffer that pain.

This was not something that could be quietly swept under the rug. It was about honouring a man's rights, about giving him the knowledge, the very fact that he had a child.

But now...

Now, Jacob had to ask himself what this honesty might cost. Heaven help him. He had so much at stake.

Nell.

Sam.

His best chance at happiness.

And he was terribly afraid that Sam's young father had the potential to take all that away from him.

Anxiety propelled him out of his chair. He marched

through the house to the back veranda and glared at the familiar view of sweeping paddocks dotted with gum trees and grazing cattle.

He knew he wouldn't be able to ignore this letter to Mitch Bradley. But right at this moment he wished that it had never arrived. Very soon, he would have to go inside to track down a phone number and ring this young man. And there was every chance that he and Nell would have to make a trip to Sydney to meet him.

Mitch Bradley might be smitten by little Sam—in fact, it was more than likely. And where would that leave Nell?

Deprived of her daughter, she'd given her whole heart to Sam. She adored him and to lose him now would be too, too cruel a blow. And to battle for him in court would be a horrendous business. Soul-destroying.

And the worst of it was that Jacob knew that he was ultimately responsible. For everything. That one unprotected act of lust all those years ago that had messed up so many lives.

What a fool he'd been then—too crazy about Nell to think straight. Problem was, he was just as big a fool now—he was still crazy about her. And he'd placed an extra burden on her by dragging her here to Koomalong.

His most foolish mistake had been thinking that if he got back together with Nell, the rest of their lives would fall into place. Happy every after. The whole damn fairy tale. As if life could be that simple, as if happiness could ever be free from the debts of the past.

With a groan of despair, he thought of the rings he'd bought on impulse when he was in Roma last week. They were in a jewellery box that he'd stowed away in the back of his wardrobe. What an idiot he'd been to think that just because Nell was spending a few weeks under his roof, she would be his forever.

He'd dragged her away from her lovely cottage, from her neighbours and friends, from the life she'd led for the past twenty years. He'd seduced her almost as soon as he'd got her under his roof and if she stopped to think about it, she would probably decide that he'd lured her to Koomalong with Sam as the bait.

Sighing heavily, burdened by the weight of his guilt, he went back into the house. He dreaded the way this might turn out, but he had no choice. He would have to find Mitch Bradley's number on the Internet...

Nell tucked a light blanket over Sam, then kissed two fingers and pressed them against his warm cheek. She tiptoed out of the room and found Jacob waiting in the hall outside. He looked dreadful. Pale despite his tan. Thinner, as if he'd lost masses of weight in the past thirty minutes.

'Have you rung Sam's father yet?' she asked.

He shook his head and she felt an instantaneous leap of hope.

'Do we really have to go through with this, Jacob?'

He smiled wearily. 'I know how you feel and I'm as worried as you are. But then I remembered something I couldn't ignore.'

'What?'

'We can't hide the truth. We'd be as bad as your parents, Nell.'

Oh, heavens. He was right. She had never been able to forgive her parents for their deception. This wasn't quite the same, but it was deception nonetheless, carrying the sins of her father into the next generation.

'How could I forget?' She gave a helpless little shake of her head. 'We can't ignore Tegan's wishes. She obviously meant Mitch to know about his son.'

'I've looked up his number,' Jacob said. 'But I was waiting for you before I called.'

She wished that he hadn't waited, but it would have sounded cowardly to say so. 'Right. I guess we'd better get it over and done with. We'll have to let Jean know what we plan to do as well.'

Heavy-hearted, she followed Jacob through to the study and sat on the deep window seat with her arms wrapped around her knees while he dialled. She watched his long fingers keying in the numbers and thought, irrelevantly, how lovely his hands were.

'Mitch?' Jacob said. 'My name's Jacob Tucker. I believe you knew my daughter, Tegan Browne. You were fruit picking with her at Beechworth last year.'

Nell had to admire how well Jacob handled his end of the conversation. It was a delicate situation, but he explained everything very smoothly and sensitively. From what she could tell, Mitch Bradley seemed to be taking the shocking news rather well.

Eventually Jacob paused. With his hand over the receiver, he looked directly at Nell. 'Mitch was shocked to hear about Tegan, but he's very excited to hear that he's a dad. He'd love to meet Sam.'

'When?' Nell asked dully.

'It's up to us. As soon as we're free.'

She felt strangely numb, as if all her emotions had been set in ice. Dropping her hands to her sides, she shrugged. 'I guess we'll have to check with the airlines and call him back.'

CHAPTER TEN

SECRETLY, Nell hoped they wouldn't be able to get flights at such short notice, but she knew that was just delaying the inevitable.

Unable to sit still and simply listen while Jacob dealt with the airlines, she went to the kitchen and made coffee for them both. When she returned to the study, her hand shook as she handed Jacob his mug.

His eyes were watchful, his jaw tight as he accepted it with terse thanks.

'Any joy with the airlines?' she asked, trying to sound a hundred times more casual than she felt.

'Actually, yes, we're in luck. There are two seats available on tomorrow's early flight out of Roma. We can be in Sydney by tomorrow afternoon.'

So soon?

How could Jacob call that luck?

Nell's stomach churned and drinking coffee was suddenly impossible. Quickly, she set the mug on his desk. 'Tomorrow's a bit soon, isn't it?'

'We don't want this hanging over our heads, Nell. We need it settled.'

The determined light in his eyes dismayed her. Was he

simply being a typical male—stoic and hiding his feelings? Or was he truly unconcerned that within twenty-four hours they could lose Sam and have their lives once again turned upside down?

'There's no point in putting this off,' he said again.

Of course, he was right. But his certainty annoyed Nell. And it frightened her. Was Jacob distancing himself now, because he thought it would all be over between them if Mitch decided to take Sam?

Worried beyond bearing, she whirled away from him, staring miserably out of the window, and saw darkness creeping through the bush, casting cold, grey shadows. The sunset was totally obscured by clouds this evening and the dusk was menacing, without any of the beauty she'd sensed on other nights. She was terribly afraid that she would burst into tears.

'I suppose you're right to be worried,' Jacob said quietly. 'If we—I mean, if you do lose Sam, it would probably make good sense for you to continue on to Melbourne after Sydney.'

Startled, she whirled back to face him. 'Are you sending me away?'

His face turned a deep red and he dropped his gaze to his coffee mug, fiddled with its handle. 'I'm just trying to be practical.'

After a moment or two, he seemed to regain his composure. Lifting his gaze once more, he looked at her with grey eyes that were carefully devoid of emotion. 'Whatever happens when we meet with Mitch tomorrow, there'll be legal issues to sort out, so it would make sense for you to continue on to Melbourne.' His gaze was sharp.

'Don't you agree, Nell?'

No, she wanted to cry. She knew that, of course, it was sensible, but right now her emotions were roiling and she had no desire whatsoever to be sensible.

She was falling apart inside. Jacob was doing everything he could to hasten her departure and that was killing her. Surely, if he loved her with the deep and overwhelming passion that she loved him, he couldn't possibly bear to be parted from her again.

Perhaps she'd been fooling herself when she'd believed that he'd wanted her at Koomalong because he loved her. It was more than likely that he'd only wanted her here as part of a package deal with Sam.

She wished she had the courage to ask those questions, but something about Jacob's frightening stillness silenced her.

Instead she agreed dully, 'I'm sure you're right. I suppose I'd better start packing.'

She held her breath and waited for him to say something—*anything*—that might offer her a tiny glimmer of reassurance. Heaven help her, a day ago he might have pulled her into his arms and murmured smiling endearments, but now he simply stood there on the other side of his desk, with his hands sunk into the pockets of his jeans, and he looked as solid and stern and stubborn as the old Brahman bull in the bottom paddock.

Giving a helpless shake of her head, Nell turned and left the room.

Nell spent the rest of the evening busily packing while Jacob remained in his study. She went between rooms, gathering up her things and Sam's. How on earth had they managed to spread so many of their belongings throughout Jacob's house? And, as she went, she could hear Jacob's deep voice as he talked on the phone, making endless arrangements with truck drivers about cattle shipments, with graziers about agistments, with stock and station agents about sales. There was even a call to Hilda Knowles asking her to care for Blue and Dander while he was away.

In fact, Jacob was so busy that he took a plate of heated leftovers back to his study and ate in snatches as he worked. Stunned and more upset than ever, Nell ate a sandwich perched on a stool at the kitchen window, staring out into the black night. Then she hurried back to her suitcases.

In his study, Jacob set down the telephone receiver and let out a weary sigh, picked up a pen and began to make tense cross-hatches on the writing pad in front of him. What a bloody awful night it had been. All evening he'd been fighting his emotions, keeping busy in a futile attempt to stop himself from thinking too hard about tomorrow. Crunch time.

By this time tomorrow night he would know the worst. The pen tore a hole in the paper. Angrily, Jacob stared at the mess he'd made on the page, quickly ripped it from the pad, balled it and binned it.

The damned thing was, the wonderful family life that he'd taken pleasure in over the past few weeks was as fragile as that paper. He and Nell had enjoyed such a short time together. They'd been the best days of his life, but now he was in danger of losing everything.

And, as far as he could see, there was not a damn thing he could do about it.

Curled in a tense ball on her side of the bed, Nell listened to the sounds of taps being turned off in the bathroom, then Jacob's soft footfall as he came across the bedroom carpet.

She felt the slight dip of the mattress as he got into bed, held her breath as he rolled towards her.

'You asleep?' he whispered.

'No.'

Her throat was tight with burning tears as she turned to him. A faint glimmer of moonlight outlined the bulk of his shoulder. His skin smelled clean and familiar and she longed to reach out, to touch him, to bury her face against his hard chest, to feel his warm embrace. But the prolonged tension of the evening had stifled the last embers of her confidence.

His hand reached through the darkness to touch her cheek.

She lay very still, hardly daring to breathe, willing him to keep touching her, to close the gap between them.

'Don't worry too much,' he said, stroking her jaw-line so gently she could barely feel it. 'I'll be with you tomorrow.'

A pitiful sob broke from her.

And, before she knew quite what was happening, he was leaning over her, lifting her hair away from her face.

'Nell,' he said once, and then he lowered his head, blocking out the moonlight, and suddenly her arms were about his neck and they were kissing and caressing and making love, swiftly overtaken by a passion so powerful she had no choice but to give in to it.

Even in their youth, they had never been this ardent, this intense. It was as if their bodies were trying to say what they hadn't managed in words.

And afterwards, when they lay in the pale shimmer of moonlight, disentangled and spent, like exhausted swimmers on the shore, Nell hoped they might talk. At last.

'I've almost broken your record,' she said lightly.

Jacob looked puzzled. 'What record is that?'

'I've stayed here for almost a month.'

'Ah...yes.' He smiled sadly.

She waited. Surely now, they could share their fears. Their hopes.

But Jacob closed his eyes and said, 'You'd better go to sleep now, Nell. We have a very early start in the morning.'

They stood on the front steps of a dilapidated flat in a suburb of Western Sydney. Nell was so nervous she thought she might be sick. Beside her, Jacob was grim-faced as he rang the doorbell.

They waited, listening while the ringing died away, for the sound of Mitch Bradley's footsteps. Nell's heart thumped. Jacob gave her back a comforting pat, but he couldn't quite manage a smile.

Hitching her bag of baby things higher on her shoulder, she held Sam more tightly. The baby grinned and cooed at her, caught a strand of her hair in his fist and pulled it towards his mouth.

'You little charmer,' she whispered, disentangling her hair gently.

Today she wished Sam wasn't quite so cute and appealing. There was a very distinct danger that Mitch would fall for him the way people so often fell for kittens and puppies in pet shops, only to find out too late they weren't able to care for them properly.

She couldn't help casting a dubious eye over the untidy flower bed beside the front steps. Apart from weeds, which were plentiful, the garden was littered with two empty soft drink cans and a screwed-up paper bag. No wonder the dusty rubber plants were struggling.

'Maybe Mitch isn't home,' she muttered hopefully when no one came to the door.

'He said he'd be here.' Jacob glanced at his watch. 'He might still be asleep.'

'At one o'clock in the afternoon?'

'He works at night in a rock band, don't forget.'

'How could I forget that?' Nell felt another nervous twist in her stomach.

Last night and today had been hideous. To her utter despair, Jacob had remained unbearably silent and withdrawn and she *still* hadn't found the courage to challenge him. Now it was too late.

'I'll try this again,' he said, lifting his hand to push the doorbell again.

'No, Jacob, wait.'

Finger poised, he frowned at her. 'We have to go through with this, Nell.'

'I know,' she said hurriedly. 'But there's something I need to ask you.'

He lowered his hand. 'What is it? What's the matter?'

She tried to moisten her parched lips. 'What will happen if we lose Sam?'

'What will happen?'

She was almost too scared to speak, but she'd been trying to get this out all day and she mustn't back down now. 'To us. We haven't talked about it and that's crazy. I can't stand it, Jacob. I have to know.'

'I—I—' His eyes glistened suddenly and his throat worked overtime. 'I thought it was settled. You'll go back to Melbourne.'

'Is that what you want?'

With an abrupt movement of his head, he looked away down the street. 'Of course it's not what I want, but I can't let what I want get in the way of your happiness. You have your friends in Melbourne. You have the theatres and book shops. Your cottage. If you lose Sam, you'll need those things. They—they'll comfort you.'

Nell swallowed the painful blockage in her throat. Her voice was shaking as she asked, 'But what about you? What if I need you more than any of those things? Where will you be?'

Slowly, Jacob turned back to her. He studied her face for five torturous long seconds and she saw realisation dawn at last, saw the beginnings of his gorgeous smile. 'Where would you like me to be?'

Before she could answer, the front door opened.

'G'day,' said a young man.

He was almost as tall as Jacob and dressed in a holey black T-shirt and ripped and faded jeans. His eyes were a sleepy blue, his hair tousled, long and blond. Blond stubble covered his jaw. He definitely looked as if he'd just rolled out of bed.

'Ah—' With obvious difficulty, Jacob dragged his eyes from Nell and offered the young man his hand. 'You must be Mitch.'

'Sure, man.' Mitch's gaze swept over them and landed on Sam and his face lit up as if someone had turned on a switch.

Nell's heart, already shaken, began a drum roll. She wanted to run away from here. She wanted to answer Jacob's question, to tell him that she wanted him to be with her, at Koomalong, anywhere, as long as they were together. And she needed to know his response.

'I'm Jacob Tucker,' Jacob said. 'And this is Nell and, of course, this is Sam.'

Mitch shook hands with them. 'Have you been waiting here long? I'm sorry, I didn't hear my alarm.'

'Not long,' Jacob assured him.

Mitch turned his attention to Sam. He took a step closer and his face softened as he stared at the baby. His Adam's apple rode up and down in his throat. 'Hey, isn't he a little dude?'

Nell smiled carefully and lifted Sam higher to give his father a better view and she wondered if they were going to be invited inside.

'Do you mind if we come in?' Jacob asked, as if reading her mind.

'Oh, sure,' Mitch replied after only the slightest hesitation. 'Come on in.' He sent a hasty glance over his shoulder and gave them a shamefaced smile. 'But the flat's pretty festy.'

As they went inside Jacob turned to Nell and smiled and she wished with all her heart she could interpret that smile. Was it saying, *Don't worry, Nell, I love you?* Or simply, *Chin up?*

At least the flat wasn't quite as bad as she'd feared. There was no lingering smell of cigarettes, which was a distinct bonus. There were dirty dishes in the sink and empty beer bottles and coffee mugs lying around, but she had to admit that it wasn't much different from the flats many of her friends had lived in when she'd been Mitch's age.

'You might like to sit over there.' Mitch pointed in the direction of an ancient vinyl settee.

Before Nell sat, she said bravely, 'Would you like to hold Sam?'

The young man gaped at her, clearly taken aback, but to his credit, he quickly recovered. 'I—I don't know.' He looked and sounded nervous. 'I've never held a baby. I'm scared I might drop him.' Then he flashed them a smile as charming as Sam's.

'That's how every guy feels when he first holds a baby,' Jacob assured him. 'Sam won't break. You'll be fine.'

'Perhaps if you sit down first,' Nell suggested. 'And then I'll hand him to you.'

'Right.' Mitch sat on the edge of an armchair that seemed to have lost its springs, his arms stiffly bent at the elbows. 'He's so little. I don't want to stuff this up.'

'You just need to have one arm under his back and make sure you support his head,' Nell explained as she gently lowered Sam into his father's arms. 'He's pretty strong now, but his head can still wobble at times.'

Mitch grinned at Sam. 'Hey, you're so tiny.' And then, 'It's me, your old man.' The baby looked up at him and smiled and Mitch laughed. 'Wow, does this kid have a cute factor off the scale, or what?'

Jacob and Nell took their seats on the settee and sat in tight-lipped silence while Mitch admired his son. His face betrayed a kaleidoscope of emotions—everything from joy, through hilarity to fear.

'He definitely looks like you,' Nell said.

'I know,' Mitch agreed. 'It's amazing, isn't it? I knew he was mine as soon as I saw him on the doorstep. It blows me away just thinking about it.' His smile vanished. 'I can't stop thinking about Tegan, though. It makes you wonder, doesn't it?' He shook his head. 'You just never know.'

She caught a distinctly misty dampness in Mitch's eyes and he quickly dropped his gaze and stared at the rust-coloured carpet at his feet.

Looking down at her hands, tightly gripped in her lap, she could hear the echo of her heartbeats drumming in her ears. Mitch Bradley was a nice guy and she felt comforted by that. For Sam's sake. And for Tegan's.

But Mitch was falling for Sam, just as she'd feared he would. She tried to squash her feelings of dismay and told herself that his interest in Sam was a good sign. Every little boy deserved his father's love and affection.

Beside her, Jacob drew a deep breath. He sat forward with his elbows propped on his knees and fixed Mitch with a steady gaze. 'I'm sorry you didn't know about Sam earlier.'

'Well, maybe that's my fault,' Mitch admitted. 'I didn't write to Tegan either. We didn't plan to hook up again, you see. It was just a—a summer thing.'

'Yes.' Jacob sent Nell a private look that told her he was remembering their own 'summer thing'.

She was so tense that she almost burst into tears.

'I'm very grateful to you both,' Mitch said. 'I needed to know about this. About Sam.'

And now it's the moment of truth, thought Nell. Any minute, Mitch was going to tell them that he and his family would take care of Sam from now on. She reached for Jacob's hand and was grateful when he enclosed her shaking fingers with his warmth and strength.

'Have you told your parents about Sam?' she asked.

Mitch shook his head. 'My parents are dead. My grandparents raised me and my sister.'

'Oh.'

A kind of awkward silence fell over them.

'So—' Nell moistened her lips. 'So, what are your plans, Mitch?'

He looked blank. 'Plans?'

'For Sam?'

'I—I don't know. What sort of plans do you mean?'

Beside her, Jacob cleared his throat. 'Let's not jump the

gun, Nell. Mitch has only just met Sam. He hasn't had a chance to think about the future.'

'Yes, I know but—' Nell saw the warning light in Jacob's eyes and stopped.

'I thought you guys were the ones with the plans,' Mitch said, clearly confused. 'You're Tegan's mum and dad. You'll be the ones raising Sam, won't you?'

Nell choked back an exclamation.

'Is that what you want?' Jacob asked quietly. 'You'd like us to continue to care for him?'

A look of panic crossed Mitch's face as his eyes flicked from Nell to Jacob. 'I didn't even think to ask you about that. I just—' He ran his tongue over his lips. 'Is there a problem? Can't you manage him any more?'

Somehow, Nell managed to stay calm. 'There's no problem, Mitch. We're quite prepared—actually, we'd be more than happy to continue to look after Sam.'

Mitch's shoulders slumped as he relaxed. 'Phew. That's a relief. You had me worried for a minute there.'

He looked down at Sam and gave a helpless shrug. 'Grandparents are so great with little kids and I wouldn't know where to start if I had to look after him. I'm only just scraping a living. And I don't know anything about nappies or feeding babies. I work crazy hours.'

'It's OK, Mitch. Stay cool.' Jacob smiled warmly at the young man, then at Nell.

'I'm not even sure how often I'll be able to see Sam,' Mitch said.

Jacob squeezed Nell's hand. 'I'm sure Nell and I will figure a way to help you to see Sam on a regular basis.'

Mitch grinned, then held Sam out to Nell. 'Can you take him while I get my camera? I'd like a shot of Sammy and me. And you two, of course. We should start a family album for the little bloke, don't you think?'

'I'll admit it now,' Nell whispered as Mitch left the room. 'I did prejudge him.'

'Forget Mitch,' Jacob said, surprising her. 'I'm more interested in the conversation we were having just before he interrupted us on the doorstep. You were going to tell me something important.'

'Oh, yes.' She cuddled Sam to her for courage. 'I was going to tell you what would have made me happy, if we weren't looking after Sam any more.'

'And I need to know the answer, Nell.'

The poor man. He couldn't have looked more serious if he were facing a firing-squad. Nell edged closer and lifted her lips close to his ear. 'I was hoping you'd let me stay with you.'

'At Koomalong?'

'Where else? Actually, I don't really care, as long as we're together.'

Jacob's face broke into a wide and radiant smile and then, in a heartbeat, he was hugging her and kissing her and squashing Sam.

'Of course I want us to be together.' He hugged her again. 'That's all I've ever wanted. I love you, Nell. And I swear I'll never let you go again.'

'Now that's a great shot,' called Mitch from the doorway.

They broke apart and Nell couldn't stop grinning. 'Jacob and I just had something to sort out.'

Mitch's cheeky smile reached from ear to ear. 'That's fine by me. I think it's absolutely cool. You old folks want to try that again? It would make a great shot for the album.'

* * *

They walked back to their car and Jacob took Nell's hand. 'Did you really mean that, Nell? That you want to stay at Koomalong?'

'You impossible man. Of course I meant it.'

'Even if we'd lost Sam?'

'Especially if we'd lost Sam.' She turned to him, her eyes huge. 'But I've been so scared that you wouldn't want me without Sam.'

'How could you think that?' Almost as soon as the question was out he knew the answer. She'd been gripped by the same uncertainties that had haunted him. He had to tell her again. 'I love you, Nell.'

'I know.' Tears sparkled in her eyes. 'I'm so happy.' The tears trembled on her eyelashes and spilled down her cheeks. 'I love you too, Jacob. So, so much.'

'But you're crying.'

'Because I'm so happy.'

They reached the car. Nell put Sam in the back and Jacob found a handkerchief and dabbed at her eyes and her cheeks. She took the handkerchief from him and blew her nose, gave him a wobbly smile.

'Let's get back to the hotel,' he said.

'Lovely.' She smiled at him. 'Actually, I'm so happy right now I would have said *lovely* if you'd suggested we swim to Africa.'

As they got into the front seats Jacob suddenly realised that *this* was the moment. There could never be a better moment. He couldn't—shouldn't—delay it a second longer.

'I have something important to ask you, Nell.'

He watched the surprise in her eyes, the swift colour in her cheeks, the soft O of her mouth.

'Here? Right now?'

'It's probably the wrong place and the wrong time. We should be down by the beautiful harbour, not stuck here on a busy road with traffic whizzing past, but I've waited too long.' Taking both her hands in his, he said, 'It's a question I asked once before. A long, long time ago.'

'Oh, Jacob. Oh, darling.'

'I haven't asked the question yet.'

'I know, but the answer is yes!' Nell slipped out of her seat belt and opened her arms to him. 'I love you,' she cried as she covered his face with kisses.

A horn blasted close by and a huge lorry rushed past them.

Looking out at the speeding traffic, Nell laughed and hugged him again. 'This is the perfect time and the perfect place. We've both waited too long for this.'

EPILOGUE

NELL looked with wonder at the tiny bundle in her arms. Her daughter was gorgeous, with a cap of dark hair and bright grey eyes.

'My tiny, shiny girl,' she whispered.

There had never been a more beautiful baby.

Nell's obstetrician had expressed concern when he'd discovered that his forty-year-old patient wanted to give birth in his country hospital. He'd tried to persuade her to go to Brisbane for her confinement, but she had insisted that she would be fine. She wasn't being sent away to the city to have *this* baby.

Her faith had been justified and Caitlin had arrived in the early hours of this morning with a minimum of fuss. Jacob had been present for the birth, holding Nell's hand, rubbing her back, giving her ice chips to suck and generally cheering her on as their perfect daughter had slipped into the world.

'Does she look like anyone we know?' he had asked as their baby girl's hand gripped his finger.

'She looks very much like Tegan,' Nell had told him. 'Which means she's going to look like you, Jacob.'

'I hope she doesn't have my ears.'

'Or your big feet.'

They had laughed together and Nell's heart had been full to overflowing—with gratitude, with happiness, with love.

Now she heard footsteps in the hospital corridor and looked eagerly towards the door, seeing Jacob's long legs and his grin stretching from ear to ear above an enormous bouquet of pink roses.

'What gorgeous roses!' She smiled up at him and thought he was still the best-looking man she'd ever seen.

'These are for both of you.' He leaned down to kiss her. 'The two loveliest girls in town.'

Setting the flowers on a bedside table, he looked down at Caitlin.

'She's beautiful, isn't she?' Nell asked for the thousandth time.

'Utterly gorgeous,' Jacob assured her.

'But you must have bought every rose in town.'

'Only every pink one,' he admitted with another happy grin.

'Thank heavens Mitch was able to come and babysit Sam,' Nell said. 'Did you get through to Koomalong? How are he and Sam?'

'I did get through and Mitch was over the moon when I told him the good news. Would you believe he stayed awake all night? Said he had no idea waiting for a baby could be so nerve-racking.'

'Poor fellow.' Nell smiled down at Caitlin. 'You were worth the wait, weren't you, sweetheart?' Quickly, she asked, 'But how's Sam?'

'He's fine. He's been a perfect lamb, according to Mitch. He's eaten an enormous breakfast and now Mitch is entertaining him with his guitar.'

'Oh, that's sweet.'

'Very sweet,' said Jacob dryly. 'I could hear Sam in the background, trying to play heavy metal on a saucepan.'

Nell groaned and smiled simultaneously.

Jacob chuckled. 'I told Mitch that was fine, as long as he doesn't get Sam started on drums.'

'Not till Caitlin's a little older,' Nell agreed. 'When's he bringing Sam in to see his little sister?'

'This afternoon.'

'I can't wait to see them together.'

Strictly speaking, Caitlin was Sam's aunt, but for the time being, as far as Nell and Jacob and the rest of the family was concerned, Sam and Caitlin were brother and sister.

'I rang everyone else,' Jacob said. 'They're all ecstatic, of course. Mum and Jean send their love and congratulations. They all want to be here for the christening.'

'It'll be just like the wedding. The whole clan at Koomalong.'

'I'll get Hilda to organise some extra household help. I don't want you overdoing things.'

'Oh, I'll be fine.'

Yes, she would be fine.

With a lump in his throat, Jacob touched his little finger to the palm of Caitlin's outstretched hand and again her fingers gripped him tightly.

He knew he was a lucky man.

'Where's my camera?' He smiled down at Nell as she relaxed against the pillows with Caitlin in her arms. 'You. Are. Glowing,' he said.

'Don't worry about the camera for now.' She patted the bed beside her. 'Come here.'

As he obeyed, she snuggled against him and lifted her

lips to the underside of his jaw. 'Just remember, my darling man—for me, nothing is perfect without you.'

With her husband beside her and her daughter in her arms, Nell breathed a sigh of utter contentment. Their dreams might have been trampled and broken when they were young, but now they had been resurrected. Bright. Shining. Coming true.

* * * * *

*Ladies, start your engines with a sneak preview
of Harlequin's officially licensed
NASCAR® romance series.*

Life in a famous racing family comes at a price

All his life Larry Grosso has lived in the shadow of
his well-known racing family—but it's now time for
him to take what he wants. And on top of that list is
Crystal Hayes—breathtaking, sweet…and twenty-
two years younger. But their age difference is creating
animosity within their families, and suddenly their
romance is the talk of the entire NASCAR circuit!

*Turn the page for a sneak preview of
OVERHEATED
by Barbara Dunlop
On sale July 29 wherever books are sold.*

Rufus, as Crystal Hayes had decided to call the black Lab, slept soundly on the soft seat even as she maneuvered the Softco truck in front of the Dean Grosso garage. Engines fired through the open bay doors, compressors clacked and impact tools whined as the teams tweaked their race cars in preparation for qualifying at the third race in Charlotte.

As always when she visited the garage area, Crystal experienced a vicarious thrill, watching the technicians' meticulous, last-minute preparations. As the daughter of a machinist, she understood the difference a fraction of a degree or a thousandth of an inch could make in the performance of a race car.

She muscled the driver's door shut behind her and waved hello to a couple of familiar crew members in their white-and-pale-blue jump suits. Then she rounded the back of the truck and rolled up the door. Inside, five boxes were marked Cargill Motors.

One of them was big and heavy, and it had slid forward a few feet, probably when she'd braked to make the narrow parking lot entrance. So she pushed up the sleeves of her canary-yellow T-shirt, then stretched forward to reach the box. A couple of catcalls came her way as her faded blue jeans tightened across her rear end. But she knew they were good-natured, and she simply ignored them.

She dragged the box toward her over the gritty metal floor.

"Let me give you a hand with that," a deep, melodious voice rumbled in her ear.

"I can manage," she responded crisply, not wanting to engage with any of the catcallers.

Here in the garage, the last thing she needed was one of the guys treating her as if she was something other than, well, one of the guys.

She'd learned long ago there was something about her that made men toss out pickup lines like parade candy. And she'd been around race crews long enough to know she needed to behave like a buddy, not a potential date.

She piled the smaller boxes on top of the large one.

"It looks heavy," said the voice.

"I'm tough," she assured him as she scooped the pile into her arms.

He didn't move away, so she turned her head to subject him to a *back off* stare. But she found herself staring into a compelling pair of green...no, brown...no, hazel eyes. She did a double take as they seemed to twinkle, multicolored, under the garage lights.

The man insistently held out his hands for the boxes. There was a dignity in his tone and little crinkles around his eyes that hinted at wisdom. There wasn't a single sign of flirtation in his expression, but Crystal was still cautious.

"You know I'm being paid to move this, right?" she asked him.

"That doesn't mean I can't be a gentleman."

Somebody whistled from a workbench. "Go, Professor Larry."

The man named Larry tossed a "Back off" over his shoulder. Then he turned to Crystal. "Sorry about that."

"Are you for real?" she asked, growing uncomfortable with the attention they were drawing. The last thing she needed was some latter-day Sir Galahad defending her honor at the track.

He quirked a dark eyebrow in a question.

"I mean," she elaborated, "you don't need to worry. I've been fending off the wolves since I was seventeen."

"Doesn't make it right," he countered, attempting to lift the boxes from her hands.

She jerked back. "You're not making it any easier."

He frowned.

"You carry this box, and they start thinking of me as a girl."

Professor Larry dipped his gaze to take in the curves of her figure. "Hate to tell you this," he said, a little twinkle coming into those multifaceted eyes.

Something about his look made her shiver inside. It was a ridiculous reaction. Guys had given her the once-over a million times. She'd learned long ago to ignore it.

"Odds are," Larry continued, a teasing drawl in his tone, "they already have."

She turned pointedly away, boxes in hand as she marched across the floor. She could feel him watching her from behind.

* * * * *

Crystal Hayes could do without her looks,
men obsessed with her looks, and guys who think
they're God's gift to the ladies.
Would Larry be the one guy who could blow all
of Crystal's preconceptions away?
Look for OVERHEATED
by Barbara Dunlop.
On sale July 29, 2008.

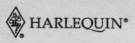

Marin Thomas
A Coal Miner's Wife
Hearts of Appalachia

High-school dropout and recently widowed
Annie McKee has twin boys to raise. The
now single mom is torn between choosing
charity from her Appalachian clan or leaving
Heather's Hollow and finding a better future
for her boys. But her handsome neighbor and
deceased husband's best friend is determined
to show the proud widow there's nothing
secondhand about love!

***Available August
wherever books are sold.***

LOVE, HOME & HAPPINESS

www.eHarlequin.com   HAR75228

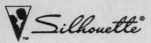

Romantic
SUSPENSE

**Sparked by Danger,
Fueled by Passion.**

Cindy Dees
Killer Affair

Seduction in the sand…and a killer on the beach.

Can-do girl Madeline Crummby is off to a remote
Fijian island to review an exclusive resort, and she hires
Tom Laruso, a burned-out bodyguard, to fly her there
in spite of an approaching hurricane. When their plane
crashes, they are trapped on an island with a serial killer
who stalks overaffectionate couples. When their false
attempts to lure out the killer turn all too real, Tom and
Madeline must risk their lives and their hearts….

**Look for the third installment
of this thrilling miniseries,
available August 2008
wherever books are sold.**

Harlequin® Historical
Historical Romantic Adventure!

From *USA TODAY*
bestselling author

Margaret Moore

A LOVER'S KISS

A Frenchwoman in London,
Juliette Bergerine is unexpectedly
thrown together in hiding with
Sir Douglas Drury. As lust and
desire give way to deeper emotions,
how will Juliette react on discovering
that her brother was murdered—
by Drury!

*Available September
wherever you buy books.*

REQUEST YOUR FREE BOOKS!
2 FREE NOVELS PLUS 2
FREE GIFTS!

HARLEQUIN ROMANCE

From the Heart, For the Heart

YES! Please send me 2 FREE Harlequin Romance® novels and my 2 FREE gifts (gifts are worth about $10). After receiving them, if I don't wish to receive any more books, I can return the shipping statement marked "cancel". If I don't cancel, I will receive 4 brand-new novels every month and be billed just $3.32 per book in the U.S. or $3.80 per book in Canada, plus 25¢ shipping and handling per book and applicable taxes, if any*. That's a savings of over 15% off the cover price! I understand that accepting the 2 free books and gifts places me under no obligation to buy anything. I can always return a shipment and cancel at any time. Even if I never buy another book, the two free books and gifts are mine to keep forever.

114 HDN ERQW   314 HDN ERQ9

Name	(PLEASE PRINT)	
Address		Apt. #
City	State/Prov.	Zip/Postal Code

Signature (if under 18, a parent or guardian must sign)

Mail to the **Harlequin Reader Service:**
IN U.S.A.: P.O. Box 1867, Buffalo, NY 14240-1867
IN CANADA: P.O. Box 609, Fort Erie, Ontario L2A 5X3

Not valid to current subscribers of Harlequin Romance books.

Want to try two free books from another line?
Call 1-800-873-8635 or visit www.morefreebooks.com.

* Terms and prices subject to change without notice. N.Y. residents add applicable sales tax. Canadian residents will be charged applicable provincial taxes and GST. Offer not valid in Quebec. This offer is limited to one order per household. All orders subject to approval. Credit or debit balances in a customer's account(s) may be offset by any other outstanding balance owed by or to the customer. Please allow 4 to 6 weeks for delivery. Offer available while quantities last.

Your Privacy: Harlequin Books is committed to protecting your privacy. Our Privacy Policy is available online at www.eHarlequin.com or upon request from the Reader Service. From time to time we make our lists of customers available to reputable third parties who may have a product or service of interest to you. If you would prefer we not share your name and address, please check here. ☐

HR08R

HARLEQUIN Romance.

Coming Next Month

**Next month in Harlequin Romance®, you're spoiled for choice!
Take your pick from a rugged rancher, a dashing prince,
an irresistible boss and a *very* mysterious stranger....**

#4039 THE RANCHER'S INHERITED FAMILY by Judy Christenberry
Western Weddings

On hiring a housekeeper, sexy Brad never expected a rabble of kids to fill his
quiet home, or that he might start to like it—and her! Sarah's never felt safer,
but she's still running from her past. How can she ask this gorgeous bachelor
to take on her unruly brood as well?

#4040 THE PRINCE'S SECRET BRIDE by Raye Morgan
The Royals of Montenevada

Prince Nico can't ignore Marisa, who is pregnant and alone. She ignites the
protective instincts Nico buried after losing his own wife and baby. But can Nico
afford to fall in love with a pregnant stranger?

#4041 MILLIONAIRE DAD, NANNY NEEDED! by Susan Meier
The Wedding Planners

Dominic and his orphaned nephew need help—and dependable Audra can
provide it. Though he knows his playboy ways could hurt Audra, every look
and touch makes him want to swap nights *out* for nights *in*—as a family.

#4042 WANTED: ROYAL WIFE AND MOTHER by Marion Lennox
By Royal Appointment

Kelly's son is heir to the throne of Alp de Ciel, and it's time for them both to
return. Though prince regent Rafael is pleased, he insists Kelly fully embrace
royal life. And, as she gets closer to Rafael, she starts to fall for the man
behind the Prince....

#4043 THE BOSS'S UNCONVENTIONAL ASSISTANT by Jennie Adams
9 to 5

Everyone knows falling for the boss is a bad idea! With her bright personality,
Sophia is completely opposite to multimillionaire workaholic Grey. Becoming
crazy about her boss is *not* what Sophia needs—but how can she resist this
broodingly handsome man?

#4044 FALLING FOR MR. DARK & DANGEROUS by Donna Alward
Heart to Heart

Tidy. Sensible. Safe. That's the kind of life that Maggie wants—until she
encounters a tall, dark and *very* dangerous stranger in her hotel. U.S.
marshall Nate offers a world of pleasure—but he has a job to do. Maggie
tries to resist him, but even a heart as closed as hers isn't immune for long.